Miguel de Unamuno

Fog

A Novel

Translated from the Spanish by Elena Barcia

Introduction by Alberto Manguel

Northwestern University Press ✦ *Evanston, Illinois*

Northwestern University Press
www.nupress.northwestern.edu

Printed in the United States of America

10   9   8   7   6   5   4   3   2   1

Library of Congress Cataloging-in-Publication Data

Names: Unamuno, Miguel de, 1864–1936, author. | Barcia, Elena,
  translator. | Manguel, Alberto, writer of introduction.
Title: Fog : a novel / Miguel de Unamuno ; translated from the Spanish by
  Elena Barcia ; introduction by Alberto Manguel.
Other titles: Niebla. English | Northwestern world classics.
Description: Evanston, Illinois : Northwestern University Press, 2017. |
  Series: Northwestern world classics |"Originally published in Spanish
  in 1914 under the title Niebla."
Identifiers: LCCN 2017015378 | ISBN 9780810135369 (pbk. : alk. paper) |
  ISBN 9780810135376 (e-book)
Subjects: LCSH: Unrequited love—Spain—Fiction. | LCGFT:
  Experimental fiction.
Classification: LCC PQ6639.N3 N513 2017 | DDC 863/.62—dc23
LC record available at https://lccn.loc.gov/2017015378

CONTENTS

Introduction   vii
    Alberto Manguel

Fog   1

Alberto Manguel

Fiction seems to be the art of questioning the possibilities of literary communication. Since Plato's *Phaedrus*, in the Socratic fable of the Pharaoh and the god Theuth, in which he had the Pharaoh object to the gift of writing because it enfeebles the art of memory, authors have tried to find ways to have it both ways: to assert fiction's ability to portray experience and, at the same time, to deny that same power. Breaking the supposed conventions of writing, betraying the naive agreements with the reader, forgoing the structural narrative grid that allows for the evolution of characters and events, abandoning documentary description and psychological analysis, storytellers from Plato onward have brought readers into the text and set interior barriers to exclude them. Though the Modernists have claimed this treacherous territory for themselves (or academics have bestowed this exclusivity upon them), the history of these tricks, strategies, and devices runs alongside the history of literature itself.

Critics have almost unanimously placed Unamuno's *Niebla* (*Fog* or *Mist*) among the great Modernist texts, next to Virginia Woolf's *The Waves* (1931) and Luigi Pirandello's *Six Characters in Search of an Author* (1921). *Niebla* precedes them all. Unamuno's novel appears as a kind of manifesto of the Modernist rebellion against what the nineteenth century considered traditional storytelling: the linear development of plot and character, an attempt to create verisimilitude through description and dialogue. Against these artifices (which Unamuno considers indulgent or immoral lies) he offers in *Niebla* a fragmenting of the story, characters denuded of physical or psychological traits, settings that are mere sketches or aleatory impressions, the whole undermined by outside voices that question, modify, or simply deny the authorial voice.

Curiously, there is little documentary evidence concerning the origins of *Niebla*. In Unamuno's vast correspondence there is a wealth of information about the conception and development of most of his other books, but hardly a word about *Niebla*, only a letter dated early in 1913 in which Unamuno mentions that he has taken up the novel "interrupted four years ago." The manuscript is dated 1907 and the version that has survived hardly differs from that of the first publication, which contains only two addenda: twenty-three lines in chapter 12 and eighteen in chapter 31.

In 1914, when Unamuno published *Niebla*, he was fifty years old. Thirteen years earlier, he had achieved what he considered the pinnacle of his career: he had been named dean for life of the University of Salamanca, where he had been holding the chair of Greek studies. His ongoing criticism of both the monarchy and the dictator Primo de Rivera would eventually lead to his destitution and banishment from which he returned in 1930, after Rivera's regime had fallen. Unamuno is therefore writing *Niebla* at the onset of World War I, in the midst of political chaos, understanding that the nineteenth-century prestige of the authorial voice could no longer be defended. Instead, he decided to try to create for his writing a complex choral narrative in which each voice breaks into several more that counterpoint one another. In the preface to *Three Exemplary Novels* (1920) he explained that a literary dialogue is in fact a conversation between six people, each character being represented by the one who he really is (known only to his Maker), the one who he is perceived as being, and the one whom he imagines himself to be. Less ambitious, Eugene O'Neill, in *Strange Interlude* (1923), divided his characters into only two: the one perceived by others and the one perceived by him- or herself.

Unamuno had already explored this deliberate fragmentation in the important essay "Whatever Comes Out" (1904), where he divided the creative process into two categories: oviparous and viviparous, the former in which the text is hatched through a lengthy process of conception and care, and the latter in which the text is born fully formed, conceived and shaped inside the author's mind. The nineteenth-century method of pouring onto the page exterior impressions of the world lacked interest for Unamuno, for whom the only possible knowledge (here the influence of his beloved Kierkegaard becomes evident) comes from within. To differentiate his work from the "exterior" writers, Unamuno called his novels *nivelas*, replacing the universal circle of the *o* with the slim intimate stroke of the *i*. According to Unamuno, nothing can be known with any certainty of the outside world; each one of us can only attempt to "know yourself" following the Socratic advice. And that deepset, secret knowledge can be shared only with the invisible Divinity. Why, then, attempt to set it down on a page, to translate into words that which, from the start, will not communicate the ineffable experience of self? Because, Unamuno suggests, literature can provide us with mirrors of our secret self, narrative frames through which readers can begin to explore their own depths. For this, fiction must abandon logic, relinquish the rational grammatical and syntactic code, crack open the text even as it is being constructed. In another fundamental essay, *The Life of Don Quixote and Sancho*, Unamuno proposes that readers accept all versions of the truth of fiction, so that, for instance, in the episode of the shaving bowl that Don Quixote takes to be a helmet, they read neither *bowl* nor *helmet* but *baciyelmo* ("bowlelmet," to coin a Carrollian portmanteau word). In this way, the fundamental ambiguity of the text, burrowing into the darkest realms of the psyche, can be preserved.

The novel's title is obviously emblematic of Unamuno's literary intentions. Unamuno liked to repeat the promise of Saint Paul, "For now we see through a glass, darkly; but then face to face: now I know in part; but then shall I know even as also I am known." Unamuno wants that the story readers will read be seen as if in a fog because, he insists, only readers can shed the necessary light that will enable them "to know as they are known." This is Unamuno's literary credo.

Fog

Prologue

Don Miguel de Unamuno insists that I write a prologue to this book of his relating the most pitiful story and mysterious death of my good friend Augusto Pérez. I have to agree, because señor de Unamuno's wishes are my commands, in the truest sense of the word. Although I never sank to the depths of Hamletian skepticism that my friend Pérez did—he came to doubt his very existence—I firmly believe that I lack what psychologists call free will. I'm somewhat comforted by the thought that Don Miguel lacks it too.

It may seem odd to some of our readers that I, a complete stranger in the world of Spanish letters, should write a prologue to one of Don Miguel's books—he being so much better known. Famous authors usually write prologues introducing their lesser-known colleagues. But Don Miguel and I have agreed to end this pernicious custom and reverse the order so that the unknown writer introduces the more famous one. Actually, most people buy books for the text rather than the prologue. So when a new writer, like me, wishes to become better known, it's natural for him to ask a veteran author to let him write a prologue instead of the other way around. This also solves one of the problems inherent in the eternal battle between the young and the old.

Besides, I have many ties to Don Miguel de Unamuno. In this novel, or *nivola*—and note that I was the one who coined the term— he relates many of the conversations I had with the unfortunate Augusto Pérez and chronicles the belated birth of my son, Victorcito. Furthermore, it seems I'm distantly related to Don Miguel. According to the expert genealogical research of my friend and renowned scholar Antolín S. Paparrigópulos, one of his ancestors and I share the same surname.

I have no idea how Don Miguel's readers will receive this nivola or what they'll think of him. For some time, I've been watching him battle his audience's naïveté, and I'm truly amazed by its depth and simplemindedness. Following the publication of a few of his articles in *Mundo Gráfico* and other similar periodicals, Don Miguel received letters and clippings of articles from provincial newspapers containing wonderful examples of the ingenuousness and dovelike innocence still found among our people. Some readers repudiated his assertion that Cervantes (Don Miguel) was often witty—apparently scandalized by his irreverence. Others were deeply moved by his melancholy reflections on trees' loss of leaves. Some were thrilled by his cry, "Make war on war!" inspired by the agonizing realization that men die even when they're not killed. Others reproduce the handful of unparadoxical truths he published after collecting them in cafés, circles, and gatherings—where they were rotting from being manhandled and reeked of the vulgarity surrounding them—by which they recognized that it was they who had uttered them. One poor fool even protested against the logomachian Don Miguel's spelling of *Kulture* with a capital *K* and his admission that even though he could invent clever phrases, he was incapable of inventing one-liners and plays on words. For this naive audience, wit and congeniality are defined by jokes and puns.

Thank goodness this guileless public seems unaware of another example of Don Miguel's mischievousness, which often goes too far—his tendency to underline words randomly in articles he's written, turning the pages upside down so that he doesn't know which words he's underlining. When he told me about this, I asked him why he did it, and he replied, "I have no idea, Victor. For fun. It's like doing a pirouette. And also because I find underlined words and italics annoying and infuriating. They're an insult to the reader; they imply he's a fool. It's like telling him, 'Pay attention, man, pay attention! This is important!' That's why I recommended to one author that he write his articles completely in italics so that his readers would understand that every word is deliberate from beginning to end. Italics turn writers into mimes, replacing intensity and tone with gestures. And notice, Victor, how the *integrista* newspapers on the far right overuse italics, small fonts, capital letters, exclamation points, and all typographical resources. Pantomime, pantomime! Nothing but pantomime! That's how crude their means of expression is, or rather how simpleminded they consider their readers. We have to put an end to this naïveté."

Other times I've heard Don Miguel declare that so-called *humorismo*, authentic humor, has barely caught on in Spain and isn't likely to catch on anytime soon. Those who call themselves humorists, he says, are sometimes satirical or ironical or just entertaining. For example, to call Taboada a humorist is to abuse the term. And there's nothing less humorous than Quevedo's biting, although clear and transparent, satire, with its obvious didacticism. Don Miguel believes that the only humorist we've had is Cervantes. He told me, "If Cervantes were to raise his head, he'd burst out laughing at those who raged because I found him witty. Most of all, he'd roar with laughter at those naive enough to take his most subtle spoofs seriously."

There's no doubt that Cervantes was mocking, seriously mocking, books about knights by imitating their language. "Barely had rosy Phoebus, and so on," which some naive Cervantes experts praise as a model of style, is but a witty parody of the baroque. And those who interpret "perforce of dawn" at the beginning of one of his chapters as an idiom failed to see that the previous chapter ended with the word "hour."

Our readers, like all unsophisticated readers, are naturally distrustful, as are our countrymen. No one wants to be mocked or ridiculed, or to be made a laughingstock. As soon as someone starts talking, we want to know what's going on and if they're joking or serious. I doubt any other nationality is as offended by the blending of truth and satire. We can't stand not knowing if something is said jokingly. The average distrustful Spaniard has a hard time realizing that something can be said both seriously and humorously at the same time, in truth and in jest, with respect for both.

Don Miguel is intrigued by the notion of tragicomedy and has told me more than once that he doesn't want to die without writing a tragic farce or a farcical tragedy—not one in which farce or the grotesque and tragedy are combined or juxtaposed, but one in which they're fused and confused. When I suggested that this was just unbridled Romanticism, he said, "Probably, but quibbling gets us nowhere. Despite having taught the classics for more than twenty years, I've never understood the idea that classicism was opposed to Romanticism. They say that the ancient Greeks distinguished, defined, and separated. Well, I like to undefine and mix things up."

Beneath all of this there's an attitude toward life I don't dare call pessimistic because I know Don Miguel dislikes that word. His mind is fixated on the monomaniacal idea that if his soul is not immortal, if no man or anything else has an immortal soul—in the sense the ingenuous Catholics of the Middle Ages believed—then nothing has inherent value and is worth pursuing. Hence, Leopardi's doctrine of ennui expressed after the demise of his great illusion: *ch'io eterno mi credea*—the belief he was eternal. This explains why Don Miguel's three favorite authors are Sénancour, Quental, and Leopardi.

But besides deepening the distrust of our people—who want to know whether or not to take things seriously—this grim, austere, and confusionistic humor annoys many Spaniards. Our countrymen want to laugh to digest their food better and forget their problems, not to regurgitate what they shouldn't have consumed and might give them heartburn—certainly not to digest their trials and tribulations. Don Miguel insists that if he provokes laughter, it's not to activate the diaphragm and aid digestion but to make his readers disgorge what they've stuffed down their throats. For we can better perceive the meaning of life and the universe on a stomach empty of sweets and excessive treats. He doesn't believe in irony without bite or in discreet humor. He says that without acerbity there's no irony, and that discretion is no friend of humor—or, as he likes to call it, ill-humorism.

All of which leads him to a most disagreeable and thankless task— one that he describes as "massaging" our people's naïveté, to see if their wit can gradually become more acute and subtle. It infuriates him to hear that our countrymen are clever, particularly in the south. "People who enjoy bullfights and find richness and pleasure in that simple spectacle are intellectual weaklings," he says, adding that there can't be a more brainless or bullheaded mentality than that of an aficionado. "Try making witty repartee with someone raving about the way Vicente Pastor has just skewered a bull!" And he despises the flamboyant style of bullfighting critics, those high priests of wordplay and ingenuous pedestrian hogwash.

Add to this Don Miguel's delight in toying with metaphysical concepts and it's easy to understand why so many dislike his writings, some because it gives them headaches, and others, believing that *sancta sancte tractanda sunt*—the sacred should be treated sacredly—feel that these concepts should never be ridiculed or mocked. To which he replies that he doesn't know why these people insist some subjects be treated more seriously than others. These protestors themselves are the spiritual offspring of those who have ridiculed the most sacred, the most comforting hopes and beliefs of their fellow human beings. If some have mocked God, why shouldn't we ridicule Reason, Science, and even Truth? And if our dearest and deepest hope has been snatched away from us, why shouldn't we mix everything up to kill time and eternity and avenge ourselves?

Some might say that this book contains lewd, even pornographic, passages, but Don Miguel has asked me to address this later in the nivola. He's ready to refute this charge and to maintain that whatever vulgarities it contains aren't meant to awaken sinful, carnal appetites. They're intended only to be an imaginative point of departure for other considerations. His disgust for all forms of pornography is well known, not only for the usual moral reasons but also because he believes that lust is what most ravages the intellect. Pornographic writers, or even simply erotic ones, seem to him the least intelligent and witty—in short, the dumbest. I've heard him say that of the three classic vices—gambling, women, and wine—the first two damage the mind more than the third. And let it be known that Don Miguel drinks only water. "You can talk to a drunk," he told me once, "and he might even say something interesting. But who can stand to converse with a gambler or a womanizer? The only thing worse than their conversations are those of bullfighting fans, the height and epitome of stupidity!"

On the other hand, I'm not surprised by this union of the erotic and the metaphysical. I seem to recall that as their literature shows, our ancestors were originally interested in war and religion and only later in eroticism and metaphysics. The worship of women coincided with the worship of subtle abstractions. In fact, during the spiritual dawn of our people in the Middle Ages, the barbarians experienced religious, even mystical, exaltation in war—the sword bears a cross on its hilt. But women occupied only a small, secondary place in their imagination. And strictly philosophical ideas lay dormant, enveloped by theology in convents' cloisters. The erotic and the metaphysical develop at the same time. Religion is warlike; metaphysics is erotic or voluptuous.

Religion is what makes us bellicose and combative, or perhaps it's combativeness that makes us religious. On the other hand, it's the metaphysical instinct, unabashed curiosity—original sin—that makes humankind sensual. Or rather it's sensuality like Eve's that awakens the metaphysical instinct—the yearning for knowledge of good and evil. And then, of course, there's mysticism, the metaphysics of religion, born of the sensuality of combativeness.

The Athenian courtesan Theodote knew this well. In his *Memorabilia*, Xenophon recounts a conversation Theodote had with Socrates. Delighted with the way the philosopher explored, or rather delivered, the truth, the courtesan asked him to become her go-between and help her "entrap" lovers. (*Syntherates*, "cohunter," is the word in the text according to Don Miguel, professor of Greek, to whom I owe this interesting, illuminating tidbit.) Throughout this fascinating conversation between the courtesan Theodote and the philosophical midwife Socrates you can clearly see the intimate relationship between both occupations—how philosophy is in large part pandering, and how pandering is also philosophical. And if this isn't true, you have to admit that at least it's ingenious, and that's good enough.

I am aware, however, that the distinction between religion and bellicosity on the one hand and philosophy and eroticism on the other will not pass muster with Don Fulgencio Entrambosmares del Aquilón, whose story Don Miguel recounted in detail in his novel, or nivola, *Love and Pedagogy*. I presume that the illustrious author of *Ars magna combinatoria* will establish a bellicose religion and an erotic religion, a bellicose metaphysics and an erotic one, a religious eroticism and a metaphysical eroticism, a metaphysical and a religious bellicosity, and a religious metaphysics, and, on the other hand, a metaphysical religion and a religious metaphysics, a bellicose eroticism and an erotic bellicosity—all of this in addition to a religious religiosity, a metaphysical metaphysics, erotic eroticism, and bellicose bellicosity. A total of sixteen binary combinations. Not to mention the ternary combinations, such as a metaphysical-erotic religion or a bellicose-religious metaphysics. But I simply don't possess Don Fulgencio's inexhaustible genius for combining, much less Don Miguel's zeal for confusion and undefining.

I have many thoughts regarding the unexpected end of this story and Don Miguel's account of the death of my unfortunate friend Augusto, an account I believe to be erroneous. I'm not going to use this prologue to dispute what happens in the text. I have to appease my conscience, however, by stating that I'm deeply convinced that Augusto Pérez carried out his intention to commit suicide, which he mentioned during our last interview, and that he took his own life in actuality and not only in imagination and desire. I believe I have undeniable proof to support this, such and so much proof as to convert opinion into fact.

And thus I end this prologue.

VICTOR GOTI

Postprologue

I would happily challenge some of the claims made by my prologue writer, Victor Goti, but since I'm privy to the secret of his—that is, Goti's, existence—I prefer to let him assume complete responsibility for what he says in his prologue. Besides, since I asked him to write the prologue and committed to accepting it in advance, that is, a priori, exactly the way it was written, it would be wrong to reject or even to correct and revise it after the fact, that is, a posteriori. However, I can't let some of his assertions stand without expressing some of my own.

I'm not sure it's proper to repeat things said in confidence to a very close friend and reveal opinions or assertions the speaker never meant to make public. In his prologue, Goti has indiscreetly disclosed some opinions of mine I never meant to share. At least I never meant for them to be related as bluntly as I expressed them in private.

Regarding his affirmation that the unfortunate . . . though why unfortunate? All right, let's assume that he was. His affirmation that the unfortunate . . . or whatever . . . Augusto Pérez committed suicide and didn't die the way I say he did—as the result of a decision I made freely—makes me smile. Some opinions deserve nothing more than a smile. My friend and prologue writer Goti should be very careful in questioning my decisions. If I find him too annoying, I'll do to him what I did to his friend Pérez. I'll let him die or kill him the way doctors kill their patients. My readers know the dilemma facing doctors: they either let a patient die because they're afraid they might kill him or they kill him off because they fear he might die on them. I'm quite capable of killing Goti if I think he might die on me, and I'm also capable of letting him die if I think I'll have to kill him off.

I have no desire to prolong this postprologue. I've said enough to offer an alternative to my friend Victor Goti, for whose work I am grateful.

M. DE U.

I

Augusto appeared at the door of his building, extended his right arm, palm down, and maintained this august, statuesque pose as he looked up at the sky. He wasn't taking command of the world, he wanted to see if it was raining. He frowned as soon as he felt the cool slow drizzle on the back of his hand. He didn't mind the drizzle, but he hated to open his umbrella. It was so elegant, so slim, neatly folded inside its cover. A closed umbrella is as elegant as an open one is ugly.

It's too bad we have to use things, Augusto thought. Use spoils and even destroys beauty. An object's most noble function is to be contemplated. An orange is so beautiful before it's eaten. This will change in heaven when our purpose is reduced—I mean expanded—to contemplate God and in Him all creation. Here, in this pathetic life, we're concerned only with using God. We expect to unfurl Him like an umbrella so that He'll protect us from all sorts of misfortune.

He bent over to roll up his pants, finally opened his umbrella, and paused for a moment. Now, which way shall I go, right or left? he wondered. Augusto didn't walk, he meandered through life. I'll wait for a dog to pass by, he thought, and continue in that direction.

It wasn't a dog that passed, however, but a beautiful young woman, whose eyes Augusto followed unwittingly. They drew him like a magnet. Street after street after street.

That boy—Augusto preferred dialoguing with himself to thinking—what's he doing there, lying face down on the ground? Probably watching an ant. Ants, hah! One of nature's most hypocritical creatures. They're always scurrying around to persuade us they're working. Like that deadbeat over there, charging ahead, elbowing everyone out of his way. I'm sure he has nothing to do. What could he possibly have to do? He's a bum. A bum just like . . . No, I'm not a bum. My imagination never rests. They're the bums, the people who pretend to work but sit around in a daze, stifling all thought. There's that stupid chocolatier rolling something in the window so that everyone can see him work. What a show-off! He's nothing but a bum. Who cares if he works or not? Work . . . work . . . hypocrisy! If you want to see real work, look at that poor cripple, dragging himself down the street. But then, what do I know?

"Excuse me, brother," Augusto said aloud. Brother? Brother in what? he wondered. In paralysis. They say we're all sons of Adam. Is this Joaquinito the son of Adam? "Good-bye, Joaquin!" Of course here's the ever-present automobile, all noise and dust. Is there any advantage to shortening distances? This obsession with travel comes from topophobia, not philotopia. People who travel all the time are running away from places, not toward them. Travel . . . travel . . . Umbrellas are such annoying gadgets. Hmm, what's this?

He stopped at the door of a building where the beautiful girl who'd been luring him with her eyes had entered. It was then Augusto realized he'd been following her. The concierge was watching him with malicious little eyes, and her gaze told Augusto what he needed to do.

This Cerbera is waiting for me to ask the name of the girl I've been following and whether she's married, he thought. Obviously, that's the next step. I could turn around and leave, but . . . No, you should always finish what you start, I hate imperfection. He put his hand in his pocket, but he had only a *duro*. It wouldn't be smart to leave and get change. He'd lose time and the moment would pass.

"Tell me, good woman," he said to the concierge—his index finger and thumb still in his pocket—"would you be so kind as to tell me confidentially, *entre nous*, the name of that young lady who just entered the building?"

"That's not a secret or anything bad, señor."

"That's why I'm asking."

"Her name is Doña Eugenia Domingo del Arco."

"Domingo? It must be Dominga."

"No, señor, Domingo. Domingo is her father's last name."

"Since she's a woman, it should be changed to Dominga. If not, where's the concordance?"

"I don't know any concordance, señor."

"And tell me"—his hand still in his pocket—"why does she go out alone? Is she single or married? Does she have parents?"

"She's single and orphaned. She lives with her aunt and uncle."

"On her father's or her mother's side?"

"I only know they're her uncle and aunt."

"That's more than enough."

"And she gives piano lessons."

"Does she play well?"

"That I don't know."

"All right, fine. Take this for your trouble."

"Thank you, señor, thank you. Is there anything else? Can I help you in any way? Would you like me to give her a message?"

"Maybe . . . maybe . . . but not now. Good-bye."

"Don't hesitate to ask, señor. You can count on my absolute discretion."

Goodness, Augusto thought as he left the concierge, now I'm obligated to this woman. It wouldn't be dignified to leave things the way they are. What would this paragon of concierges think of me? So . . . Eugenia Dominga, I mean Domingo, del Arco? Good. I'll make a note of it so I won't forget. There's no better mnemonic device than a notebook in your pocket. That's what the unforgettable Don Leoncio would say: "Don't fill your head with something that'll fit in your pocket." Of course, the opposite is also true: "Don't fill your pocket with something that'll fit in your head." That concierge . . . what's her name?

He took a few steps back.

"One more thing, good woman."

"Of course."

"What's your name?"

"Mine? Margarita."

"Good, very good. Thank you."

"You're welcome."

Augusto set off again, arriving a short time later at the Paseo de la Alameda. It had stopped drizzling. He closed his umbrella, folded it, and put it inside its cover. Then he approached a bench. When he touched it, it felt wet, so he opened a newspaper, spread it, and sat down. Next he took out his notebook and held up his fountain pen. This is a very useful gadget, he thought, otherwise I'd have to write down that girl's name in pencil and it could get erased. Will her image be erased from my memory? What does she look like? What does the sweet Eugenia look like? I remember only her eyes. I feel the touch of those eyes. As I rambled on poetically, a pair of eyes gently tugged at my heart.

Let's see. Eugenia Domingo . . . yes, Domingo . . . Del Arco. Domingo? I can't get used to her name being Domingo. She'll have to change her name to Dominga. What about our sons? Will their second surname be Dominga? I'm sure they'll drop my name, this undignified "Pérez," and shorten it to a P. Will our eldest son be named Augusto P. Dominga? Where is this wild fantasy taking me? He jotted down in his notebook "Eugenia Domingo del Arco, Avenida de la Alameda 58." Above her name there were two heptasyllables:

From the cradle comes sadness
And from the cradle comes joy

My goodness, Augusto thought, this piano teacher, Eugenia, cut short the excellent beginning of a transcendent lyrical poem. She interrupted it. Interrupted? We look to the events and vicissitudes of life to feed our innate sadness or joy. The same situation can be happy or sad depending on our temperament. What about Eugenia? I have to write to her. But not here, at home. Should I go to the club? No, home. These kinds of things should be done at home. Home? My house is not a home, more like an ashtray. Oh, my Eugenia!

And Augusto headed back to his apartment.

II

When the servant opened the door . . .

Augusto was alone in the world and wealthy. His elderly mother had died barely six months before these trivial events. He lived with a male servant and a cook, longtime employees and the offspring of others who'd served there before them. The servant and cook were married to each other but had no children. When the servant opened the door, Augusto asked if he'd had any visitors.

"None, señor."

The question and answer were part of a routine. Augusto rarely had visitors.

He entered his study, grabbed an envelope, and wrote, "Miss Eugenia Domingo del Arco, to be delivered to her personally." With the blank paper in front of him, he propped his elbows on the desk, lowered his head between his hands, and closed his eyes. First let's think about her, he said to himself.

In the darkness, he tried hard to recapture the radiance of those eyes that had accidentally drawn him to her. He spent a while conjuring the image of Eugenia. Since he'd caught only a glimpse of her, he had to use his imagination. As he strained to evoke her image, a vague figure shrouded in dreams began to take shape in his mind . . . and he fell asleep. The night before had been difficult, filled with insomnia.

"Señor!"

"Yes?" he woke up.

"Your lunch is ready."

Was it the servant's voice or hunger, echoing through that voice that awakened him? Psychological mysteries! These were Augusto's thoughts as he walked to the dining room, muttering, "Oh, psychology!"

He enjoyed his daily lunch: a couple of fried eggs, steak, potatoes, and a slice of Gruyère. Afterward, he drank his coffee and relaxed in his rocking chair. He lit a cigar, raised it to his lips, and whispering, "Oh, my Eugenia," began to think of her.

My Eugenia, yes, mine, he thought. The one I'm creating, not the concierge's. Not the flesh-and-blood one who accidentally appeared in front of my building. Accidentally appeared? What appearance isn't accidental? What's the logic behind appearances? The same as that behind the figures created by my cigar's clouds of smoke. Randomness! Randomness is the deep rhythm of the world, randomness is the soul of poetry. My random Eugenia! My placid, routine, and humble life is a Pindaric ode woven from a thousand daily trifles. The everyday . . . Give us this day our daily bread. Give me, oh Lord, a thousand daily trivialities. We don't succumb to the great joys and sorrows of life because they are cloaked in an enormous fog of small incidents. That's what life is: a fog. Life is a nebula. Eugenia emerges from it now. And who is Eugenia? I realize I've been looking for her for some time, and while I was looking, she appeared right in front of me. Isn't this the same as finding something? When the thing you're looking for finally appears, doesn't it appear because it's moved by the search? Didn't America search for Columbus? Didn't Eugenia search for me? "Eugenia! Eugenia! Eugenia!"

Augusto found himself calling out Eugenia's name. His servant, passing by the dining room, heard him shout and entered the room.

"You called, señor?"

"I didn't call *you*. But listen, your name's Domingo, isn't it?"

"Yes, señor," the servant replied, not at all surprised by the question.

"And why is your name Domingo?"

"Because that's what people call me."

Good, very good, thought Augusto. Our name is what people call us. In Homeric times people and things had two names, one given by their fellow man and one given by the gods. What does God call me? And why shouldn't I have a different name from the one people call me? Why shouldn't I give Eugenia a name that's different from what others call her, from what the concierge, Margarita, calls her? What shall I call her?

"You can go," he told the servant.

Augusto got up from the rocking chair, went to his study, picked up a pen, and began to write:

Señorita: This morning, beneath the sky's gentle drizzle, you accidentally appeared in front of the building where I live but no longer have a
home. When I became aware of what I was doing, I went to the door of
your house. I don't know if it's your home. I was drawn there by your
eyes—two luminous stars in the haze of my world. Forgive me, Eugenia, and allow me to call you by this sweet name. Forgive my poetic
language. I live in a constant, infinitely poetic state.

I don't know what else to say. Actually, I do, but there is so much,
so much I have to say to you, that I think it's better to wait until we can
meet and talk.

That's what I want now, for us to meet and talk, to write to each other and get to know each other. Later, God and our hearts will decide.
Will you, Eugenia, sweet apparition in my everyday life, will you lend
me your ears?

Surrounded by the fog of my life, I await your response.

Augusto Pérez

He signed his name with a flourish thinking, I like this custom of
signing your name with a flourish because it's so pointless. He sealed
the letter and walked out onto the street again.

Thank God, he thought on his way to Avenida de la Alameda.
Thank God I know where I'm going and that I have someplace to go.
This Eugenia of mine is a blessing from God. She's already provided
a destination, an end for my wanderings. I now have a house to go
to and a confidant in the concierge.

As he continued down the street talking to himself, he crossed
paths with Eugenia without even noticing the radiance of her eyes.
The spiritual fog was too thick. But Eugenia noticed him. Who's this
young man? she wondered. He's very good-looking and seems well-
off. Almost unconsciously, she sensed he was someone who'd followed her that morning. Women always know when you're looking
at them, even if you don't really see them, and when you see them
without really looking.

Augusto and Eugenia continued walking in opposite directions,
their souls cutting through the tangled spiritual web of the street.
The street is a fabric woven from looks of desire, envy, disdain, compassion, love, and hatred, from old words whose spirit has hardened,

from thoughts and yearnings—a mysterious fabric that envelops the souls of all who pass by.

At last Augusto found himself again before a smiling Margarita, the concierge. The first thing she did when she saw him was take her hand out of her apron's pocket.

"Good afternoon, Margarita."

"Good afternoon, señor."

"Call me Augusto."

"Don Augusto," she added.

"Some names shouldn't have a Don before them," he said. "Just as there's a huge difference between Juan and Don Juan, there's an equally big one between Augusto and Don Augusto. But, never mind. Has señorita Eugenia gone out?"

"Yes, a few minutes ago."

"Which way did she go?"

"That way."

Augusto started walking in that direction but soon returned. He'd forgotten the letter.

"Señora Margarita, would you please deliver this letter to señorita Eugenia's own snow-white hands?"

"I'd be happy to."

"To her own snow-white hands, understand? Those hands as ivory-white as the keys of the piano they caress."

"Yes, I've done this before."

"What do you mean, you've done this before?"

"Does the gentleman think this is the first letter of its kind?"

"Of its kind? Do you know what kind of letter this is?"

"Of course. Just like the others."

"Just like the others? What others?"

"The young lady has had quite a few suitors."

"Is she free at the moment?"

"At the moment? No. She has something like a fiancé, although I think he's still just vying for the position. She could be testing him. He might be temporary."

"Why didn't you tell me?"

"You didn't ask."

"You're right. Anyway, give her this letter. Put it into her own hands, understand? We'll fight! Here's another *duro* for you."

"Thank you, señor, thank you."

It was hard for Augusto to leave. He was beginning to enjoy Margarita the concierge's hazy daily conversations. Maybe it was a good way to kill time.

We'll fight, Augusto thought as he walked down the street. Yes, we'll fight. So she has a boyfriend, another potential suitor? We'll fight! *Militia est vita hominis super terram.*

My life now has a purpose, I have to win someone over. Oh, Eugenia, my Eugenia! You'll be mine. Well, at least *my* Eugenia will be mine. The one I've created from the brief glimpse of those eyes, from those two stars in my nebula. This Eugenia will be mine. The other can be the concierge's or whoever's. We'll fight! We'll fight and I'll win. I have the secret to victory.

Oh, Eugenia, my Eugenia!

And he found himself at the door of the club, where Victor was waiting to begin their daily round of chess.

III

"You're late today," Victor said. "You're usually so punctual."

"You know how it is. I'm busy."

"Busy . . . you?"

"Do you think only stockbrokers are busy? Life is a lot more complicated than you can imagine."

"Or I'm less complicated than you think."

"Anything's possible."

"All right. Your move."

Augusto advanced the king's pawn two squares, but instead of humming bits of opera as he usually did, he thought, Eugenia, my Eugenia, purpose of my life, sweet radiance of twin stars in the fog. We'll fight! There's definitely logic in this game of chess. And yet, how nebulous, how unpredictable after all. Maybe logic is also accidental and random. My Eugenia appearing like that . . . Could there be logic in it? Maybe it's part of a divine game of chess.

"Come on," Victor interrupted. "Didn't we say that we couldn't take back any moves? You touch it, you play it."

"Yes, that's what we agreed," Augusto said.

"If you make that move, I'll take your bishop."

"You're right, I was preoccupied."

"Well, focus. A game of chess isn't a walk in the park. Remember, you touch it, you play it."

"Right. There's no going back."

"That's how it should be. That's why this game is so educational."

Why shouldn't you be distracted while you play? Augusto wondered. Isn't life a game? Why shouldn't you be able to take back certain moves? So much for logic. The letter might already be in Eugenia's hands. *Alea iacta est!* What's done is done. What about tomorrow? Tomorrow is in God's hands. And yesterday? Whose hands is yesterday in? Oh, yesterday, treasure of the strong! Blessed yesterday, essence of the fog of daily life.

"Check!" Victor interrupted again.

"You're right, you're right. Let's see. How have I let things get this far?"

"By daydreaming, as usual. If you weren't so distracted, you'd be one of our best players."

"So tell me, Victor, is life a game or a distraction?"

"The game itself is only a distraction."

"Then what difference does it make if you're distracted in some way?"

"If you're going to play, play well."

"Why not play badly? And what does it mean to play well or badly anyway? Why not move these pieces in other ways?"

"That's the theory, that you, Augusto, my friend and eminent philosopher, have taught me."

"Well, I have some very good news."

"Tell me."

"Prepare to be amazed, my friend."

"I'm not one to be amazed a priori or beforehand."

"Well, here goes. Do you know what's happening to me?"

"That your head is increasingly in the clouds?"

"It just so happens that I've fallen in love."

"Hah! I already knew that."

"What do you mean, you already knew?"

"Of course. You are in love *ab origine*, since birth. You have an innate infatuation."

"It's true that love is born with us at birth."

"I didn't say love, I said infatuation. I already knew, without you telling me, that you were in love, or rather . . . smitten. I knew it better than you."

"But with whom? Tell me, with whom?"

"You don't know that any more than I do."

"Well, look, maybe you're right."

"I told you. So, is she blond or brunette?"

"The truth is I don't know, I imagine she's neither. That's it, she has light-brown hair."

"Is she tall or short?"

"I don't remember that either. Probably average. But what eyes, Victor, what eyes my Eugenia has."

"Eugenia?"

"Yes, Eugenia Domingo del Arco, Avenida de la Alameda 58."

"The piano teacher?"

"That's her, but . . ."

"I know who she is. And now . . . check again!"

"But . . ."

"Check," I said.

"All right."

Augusto defended his king with a knight . . . and he ended up losing the game.

As they were parting, Victor put his arm around Augusto's neck like a yoke and whispered in his ear, "So, Eugenita the pianist, eh? Good, Augustito, good. You'll inherit the earth."

Those diminutives, Augusto thought, those awful diminutives! And he walked out onto the street.

IV

Why are diminutives signs of affection? Augusto wondered on his way home. Does love somehow shrink the beloved? Me, in love? In love! Who would have thought? But . . . is Victor right? Am I in love *ab initio*? Maybe my love preceded the beloved. Actually, this love summoned the beloved and drew her out of creation's fog. But if I advance that rook, he can't checkmate me, he can't. And what is love anyway? Who defined love? Once you define it, it isn't love anymore. Christ, why does the mayor allow such ugly lettering on shops? That bishop was badly played. And how can I have fallen in love when, strictly speaking, I can't even say I know her? Of course, I'll get to know her later. Love precedes familiarity, and familiarity kills love. *Nihil volitum quin praecognitum.* Father Zaramillo taught me that. But I've reached the opposite conclusion: *nihil cognitum quin praevolitum.* They say that to know is to forgive. But no, to forgive is to know. First love, then familiarity. Why didn't I see that checkmate coming? What does it take to fall in love? A glimpse, just a glimpse. That's love's intuition, a glimpse in the fog. Later the details emerge—the perfect vision. The fog turns into drops of water or hail, or snow, or stones. Science is a hailstorm. No, a fog, a fog! Oh, to be an eagle soaring across the slopes of the clouds and to see the sun through them, a nebulous light.

The eagle! What might the eagle of Patmos have said to Minerva's owl when he fled from Saint John and ran into the owl escaping from Olympus? The eagle of Patmos can gaze directly at the sun but is blind in the darkness, and Minerva's owl can see in the blackest night but can't look at the sun.

At this point Augusto crossed paths with Eugenia but didn't notice her. Knowledge comes later, he thought. What was that? I could have sworn I saw two luminous and mystical stars cross my path. Could it have been her? My heart tells me . . . Never mind, I'm home now.

He entered the apartment. Approaching his bedroom, he looked at the bed. Alone, he thought. Sleep alone, dream alone. When two people sleep together, they probably share the same dream. Mysterious emanations probably join their minds. Or maybe the closer two hearts become, the more distant their minds become? Maybe. Maybe they're in mutually adverse positions. If two lovers think alike, they feel the opposite. If they share the same loving feeling, each thinks differently from the other, maybe even the opposite. A woman loves only a man who thinks differently from her—that is, a man who thinks. Let's see what this venerable couple has to say.

Many nights before going to bed, Augusto played a game of *tute* with his servant, Domingo, while Domingo's wife, the cook, looked on.

They began to play.

"Twenty in hearts!" Domingo exclaimed.

"Tell me," Augusto said suddenly, "what if I were to get married?"

"That would be wonderful, señorito," Domingo said.

"That depends," Liduvina, his wife, dared to remark.

"Didn't you get married?" Augusto asked her.

"That depends," she replied.

"What do you mean, that depends? Tell me."

"Getting married is easy enough, but being married is not so easy."

"That's just popular wisdom, the source of . . ."

"And what your future wife is like . . ." Liduvina continued, afraid that Augusto was about to launch into one of his monologues.

"What about her? What about the woman who is to become my wife? Come on, say it! Say it, woman!"

"Well, since the señorito is so good . . ."

"Go on, woman, say it once and for all!"

"Remember what our dear lady used to say."

At the reverential mention of his mother, Augusto put his cards down on the table and paused for a moment. Many times his mother, that sweet woman and daughter of misfortune, had said to him, "I can't live much longer, my son. Your father is calling me. Maybe he needs me more than you do. As soon as I leave this world and you're alone, get married. Marry as soon as possible. Bring a mistress and lady to this house. It's not that I don't trust our old faithful servants, but bring a mistress to the house. Let her be a true mistress, my son. Give her the keys to your heart, your fortune, your pantry, your kitchen, and your decisions. Look for a woman who knows how to manage things, who knows how to love . . . and manage you."

"My wife will play the piano," Augusto said, shaking off his memories and his nostalgia.

"The piano? What good is that?" Liduvina asked.

"What good is that? That's its greatest charm, that it serves no useful purpose. I'm sick of everything having to be useful."

"Are you sick of us?"

"No, not you. Besides, a piano serves a purpose. It fills homes with harmony and prevents them from being mere ashtrays."

"Harmony? How can you live on that?"

"Liduvina, Liduvina . . ."

The cook lowered her head following this gentle reprimand, as she always did.

"Of course she'll play the piano. She's a piano teacher," Augusto said.

"Then she won't play it," Liduvina said firmly. "Why else would she get married?"

"My Eugenia . . ." Augusto began.

"Oh, her name is Eugenia, and she's a piano teacher?" the cook said.

"Yes. So what?"

"The one who lives with her aunt and uncle on Avenida de la Alameda, above Mr. Tiburcio's shop?"

"Yes. Do you know her?"

"Yes, by sight."

"No, there's more, Liduvina, there's more. Tell me. It concerns my future and my happiness."

"She's a nice girl. Yes, she's nice."

"Come on, Liduvina, tell me. Think of my mother!"

"Remember her advice, señor. Who's that in the kitchen? I'll bet it's the cat!"

The cook stood up and left the room.

"Do you want to finish the game?" Domingo said.

"Of course. We can't leave the game like this. Whose turn is it?"

"Yours, señor."

"Well, here goes."

He lost this game, too, because he was distracted.

My goodness, he thought on the way to his bedroom, everyone knows her, everyone but me. This is how love works. What about tomorrow? What shall I do tomorrow? Never mind. One day at a time. Now to bed.

And he lay down.

But once in bed he continued mulling things over. The truth is that for two terrible years since my blessed mother died I've been bored without even knowing it, he thought. You can be bored without even realizing it. Almost all men are unconsciously bored. Boredom is at the core of life, and boredom is responsible for the invention of games, distractions, novels, and love. The fog of life exudes a sweet boredom, a bittersweet liqueur. All these insignificant daily events, these pleasant conversations that kill time and prolong our lives, what are they if not the sweetest boredom? Oh, Eugenia, my Eugenia, jewel of my life's unconscious boredom. Help me in my dreams. Dream in me and of me.

And he fell asleep.

V

A magnificent eagle soared through the clouds, his powerful wings glowing with dew, his predatory eyes fixed on the solar haze, his heart resting in sweet ennui, secure in a breast tempered by storms. Around him, the silence created by remote murmurs from the earth, and above, at the highest point in the sky, two twin stars poured invisible balm. A shrill cry of "*La Correspondencia!*" broke through the silence, and Augusto opened his eyes to the light of a new day.

Am I dreaming or living? he wondered, pulling the blanket tightly around him. Am I an eagle or a man? What's in that newspaper today? What news will the new day bring? Will an earthquake have swallowed Corcubión last night? Why not Leipzig? Ah, the lyrical association of ideas, the Pindaric disorder. The world is a kaleidoscope. Man imposes logic, but randomness is the most supreme of all the arts. So . . . let's sleep a little longer. He rolled over in bed.

"*La Correspondencia!*" Then the vinegar merchant! Then a carriage, then a car, and then young boys. Impossible, Augusto thought. I'm surrounded by life again. And with it, love. And what is love? Isn't it the distillation of everything? Isn't it the juice we extract from the tedium? Let's think about Eugenia. This is a perfect time.

He closed his eyes so he could think about Eugenia. Think? But his thoughts began to fade, to melt away, and shortly all that remained was a polka. An organ grinder was playing beneath his bedroom window, and Augusto's soul was ringing with notes, not thoughts.

The essence of the world is musical, Augusto thought as the organ's last note faded. And isn't my Eugenia also musical? All laws are based on rhythm, and the rhythm is love. On this divine morning, the most unsullied time of day, I've had a revelation: love is the rhythm.

Mathematics is the science of rhythm; music is the sensuous expression of love. The expression, not its realization, let's be clear.

He was interrupted by a gentle knock on the door.

"Come in."

"You called, señor?" Domingo said.

"Yes, it's time for breakfast."

He had called out inadvertently, at least an hour and a half earlier than usual. Once he'd called out, he had to ask for his breakfast, even though it was too early.

Love awakens and sharpens the appetite, he thought. You have to live to love, and you have to love in order to live. He got up to have his breakfast.

"What's the weather like, Domingo?"

"The same as always, señor."

"Neither good nor bad?"

"Exactly."

This was the servant's theory, for he, too, had his theories.

Augusto washed, combed his hair, got dressed, and groomed like someone who now had a purpose—bursting with a zest for life, though still a bit melancholy.

He walked out onto the street but soon felt his heart pound in his chest. Hold on, he thought. I *have* seen her. I've known her for a long time. Her image is almost innate in me. Mother, help me! As they crossed paths and Eugenia passed by his side, he greeted her more with his eyes than with the tip of his hat. He was about to turn around and follow her, but good sense prevailed, as well as his desire to talk to the concierge.

It's her, yes, it's her, he thought. One and the same, the one I've been in search of for years, even if I didn't know it, and she's been searching for me. We were destined for each other in a preordained harmony. We're two monads that complement each other. The family is the true social cell. I'm nothing but a molecule. My God, science is so poetic! Mother, look down on your son. Give me some advice from heaven. Eugenia, my Eugenia!

He realized he was hugging the air and glanced around in case someone was watching him. Love is a kind of ecstasy, he thought. It takes us out of ourselves. Then he was brought back to reality . . . reality? . . . by Margarita's smile.

"Do you have any news for me?" Augusto asked.

"None, señor. It's still too soon."

"Did she ask any questions when you gave her the letter?"

"Nothing."

"How about today?"

"Today she did. She asked me for your address, whether I knew you and who you were. She said you'd forgotten to include your address, and then she asked me to do something for her."

"Do what? What is it? Tell me."

"She said that if you came back, I was to tell you that she's engaged, that she has a fiancé."

"She has a fiancé?"

"That's what I said, señor."

"It doesn't matter. We'll fight!"

"All right, we'll fight."

"Can I count on your help, Margarita?"

"Of course."

"Then we'll win."

He left and walked to the Alameda to calm his spirit with the beautiful greenery and birds singing love songs. His heart grew young again, and winged memories of his childhood sang like nightingales inside him. A sky full of memories of his mother showered a sweet liquid light over all his other recollections.

He hardly remembered his father, a mythical shadow lost in the distance, a bloodstained cloud at dusk. Bloodstained because as a child he had seen him, pale as a corpse, covered in the blood he'd vomited. Augusto's heart still echoed, so many years later, with his mother's cry of, "Son!" which tore through the house, a cry he wasn't sure was meant for his dying father or for himself, hopelessly bewildered by the mystery of death.

A short while later, his mother, trembling with grief and repeating, "My son! My son!" clasped him to her breast and baptized him with fiery tears. And he cried too, pressing himself against her, not daring to turn his head or leave the sweet darkness of that heaving bosom for fear he would see the bogeyman's hungry eyes. Many days of weeping and blackness followed, until the tears no longer flowed outwardly and the darkness in the house began to fade.

It was a sweet, warm house. Light filtered through the curtains embroidered with white flowers. The armchairs embraced you like grandparents who'd become childlike with the years. There was the ashtray with the ashes from the last cigar his father had smoked. And there, on the wall, a portrait of the two of them, his father and his mother, now a widow, painted the day they were married. He was a tall man, seated with one leg crossed over the other, with the tongue of his boot showing. She, much shorter, stood by his side, resting her hand on her husband's shoulder—a delicate hand that seemed made to pose like a dove rather than clasp anything.

His mother came and went silently like a small bird, always dressed in black, with a smile tinged with the sadness of those first few days of widowhood—traces of which appeared on her lips and around her searching eyes. "I have to go on living for you, only for you, Augusto," she said before going to bed at night. His dreams began with her kiss, still damp with tears. Their life continued like a sweet dream.

His mother read to him in the evening, sometimes an account of a saint's life, other times a novel by Jules Verne or a simple short story. Sometimes she even laughed, silently and sweetly, leaving behind her distant tears.

Once he started school, his mother helped him with his lessons, studying in order to keep up with him. She studied the strange names in world history and used to smile and say, "My God, the atrocities men have committed!" She studied mathematics, and it was in this that his sweet mother excelled. "If my mother were to devote herself to mathematics . . ." Augusto would say, recalling her fascination with factoring a second-degree equation. She studied psychology and this was her hardest subject. "Why make everything so complicated?" she'd ask. She studied physics and chemistry and natural history. But she didn't like the strange names people gave animals and plants. Physiology horrified her, and she gave up going over her son's lessons in it. Just looking at the illustrations of the heart or the lungs reminded her of the blood-soaked death of her husband. "This is very unpleasant, son," she'd say. "Don't study medicine. It's best not to know what's inside you."

When Augusto graduated from high school, she hugged him, stared at the down on his upper lip, burst into tears, and exclaimed, "If only your father were alive!" She made him sit on her lap, which embarrassed him, since he was a young man, and held him there silently, staring at her late-husband's ashtray.

Then came college, new friends, and his mother's wistfulness as she watched her son spread his wings. "I live for you, I live for you," she'd repeat. "And for whom will you live? It's the way of the world, my son."

When they returned home the day he graduated from law school, she kissed his hand in a comically serious way. Then she hugged him and whispered in his ear, "May your father bless you, my son."

His mother never went to bed before he did, and she always tucked him in with a kiss. He was never able to stay up very late. She was the first thing he saw when he woke up, and when they ate, she wouldn't eat anything he wouldn't eat.

They often went out for walks together, strolling along in silence beneath the sky, she thinking of her late husband and he of the first thing that caught his eye. She would bring up the same subjects again and again, everyday things, very old things that were somehow always new. Often she would began with, "When you get married . . ." And whenever a beautiful or even a pretty girl passed by, his mother would glance at Augusto out of the corner of her eye.

Death came gradually, gravely, sweetly and painlessly. It tiptoed in silently, like a migrating bird, and carried her slowly away one fall afternoon. She died holding her son's hand, gazing into his eyes. Augusto felt her hand grow cold, saw her eyes grow still. He gave her chilly hand a warm kiss, released it, and closed her eyes. He knelt by her bed, awash in the memories of their unvarying years together.

And now he was here, in the Alameda, listening to the birds chirp above him and thinking about Eugenia. And Eugenia had a fiancé. "I'm afraid of what might happen the first time you find a thorn in life's path, my son," his mother would say. If only she were here to transform this thorn into a rose.

If my mother were alive, she would find a way to solve this problem, Augusto thought. After all, it's no harder than a second-degree equation. And really, in the end, it *is* a second-degree equation.

His soliloquy was interrupted by a faint whimpering, like that of an animal in distress. He looked around and discovered a forlorn puppy in the middle of a thicket, trying to find his way out. Poor little guy, he thought. They've left a newborn puppy here to die. They

didn't have the courage to kill it. He picked it up. The dog was looking for his mother's nipple.

Augusto stood up and began to walk home. When Eugenia finds
out about this, my rival won't have a chance, he thought. She's going
to fall in love with this pitiful little dog. He's so cute. Poor thing, he
can't stop licking my hand.

"Bring some milk, Domingo, bring it right away," he said as soon
as his servant opened the door.

"I can't believe you bought a dog, señor."

"I didn't buy him, Domingo. This dog isn't a slave. He's free. I
found him."

"Yes, of course, he's a foundling."

"We're all foundlings, Domingo. Bring the milk."

He brought the milk and a small sponge to help the puppy suck
it. Then Augusto asked him to bring a baby bottle for Orfeo. That
was the name he gave him. No one, including Augusto, knows why.
From that day on, Orfeo became the audience for his soliloquies and
the one to whom he confided his secret love for Eugenia.

"Look, Orfeo," he said quietly. "We have to fight. What do you
think I should do? If only my mother had known you. But you'll see.
You'll see when you sleep in Eugenia's lap, under her sweet, warm
hand. What should we do now, Orfeo?"

Lunch that day was melancholy, as was his walk, his chess game,
and his dream that night.

VI

I have to make a decision, Augusto thought, as he paced in front of the building on Avenida de la Alameda 58. Things can't go on like this. Just then a door opened on the second floor balcony—the floor where Eugenia lived—and out came a gaunt, gray-haired woman holding a birdcage. She was about to hang her canary in the sun, but the nail on the wall gave way and the cage fell down to the sidewalk. The woman cried out in despair, "Oh, my Pichín!" and Augusto rushed to pick up the cage with the terrified canary flapping inside it. He climbed the stairs to the apartment with the canary still fluttering in its cage. He could feel his heart pounding inside his chest. The lady was waiting for him.

"Oh, thank you, señor! Thank you!"

"Thank *you*, señora."

"My Pichín, my Pichincito, settle down now! Would you like to come in, señor?"

"I'd love to, señora."

Augusto entered the apartment. The woman led him to the drawing room and then left him alone, saying, "Wait just a minute, I'm going to put my Pichín away."

Just then an elderly gentleman entered the room, probably Eugenia's uncle. He was wearing tinted glasses and a fez upon his head. He approached Augusto, sat down next to him, and proceeded to utter a phrase in Esperanto that means, "Don't you agree that, thanks to Esperanto, we'll soon achieve world peace?"

Augusto thought about fleeing, but his love for Eugenia restrained him. The man continued speaking in Esperanto and Augusto finally decided to respond.

"I don't understand a word you're saying, señor."

"He's probably speaking that damned gibberish they call Esperanto," the aunt said as she entered the room. "Fermín, this is the canary man."

"That makes as little sense to me as you say I do when I speak Esperanto," her husband replied.

"This man picked up my poor Pichín when he fell into the street and was kind enough to return him to me." She turned to Augusto. "What's your name, señor?"

"I'm Augusto Pérez, señora, son of the late widow of Pérez Rovira. Perhaps you knew her?"

"Doña Soledad?"

"Yes, Doña Soledad."

"I knew the good lady quite well. She was an exceptional widow and mother. I congratulate you."

"I congratulate myself. I owe this meeting to your canary's lucky accident."

"Lucky? You call it lucky?"

"Lucky for me."

"Thank you, señor," Don Fermín said. "Men and their affairs are ruled by enigmatic laws, but we can catch glimpses of them. I have my own particular ideas about nearly everything . . ."

"Not that broken record again!" the aunt said. "How were you able to rescue my Pichín so quickly?"

"I'll be honest with you, señora. The truth is that I was loitering around the building."

"This building?"

"Yes. You have a charming niece."

"Say no more, señor. Now I understand why the accident was lucky and I see that canaries can be providential."

"Who among us knows the ways of Providence?" said Don Fermín.

"I know them," his wife said. She turned to Augusto. "You're a welcome visitor to this house. That goes without saying. You're Doña Soledad's son. Besides, you're going to help me get a ridiculous whim out of that girl's head."

"What about free will?" Don Fermín said.

"Oh, hush. Keep your anarchism to yourself."

"Anarchism?" Augusto said.

Don Fermín's face lit up and he replied softly, "Yes, señor, I'm an anarchist, a mystical anarchist. Only in theory, you understand, in theory . Don't be afraid, my friend." As he spoke, he placed his hand gently on Augusto's knee. "I don't throw bombs. My anarchism is purely spiritual because, my friend, I have my own ideas about almost everything."

"Are you an anarchist too?" Augusto asked the aunt, just to say something.

"Me? That business of nobody being in charge is nonsense. Someone has to be in charge. If no one's in charge, who's going to obey? Don't you understand it's impossible?"

"Oh, ye of little faith who say it's impossible—" Don Fermín began.

But the aunt interrupted, "All right, Don Augusto, we have a deal. You seem to be a wonderful person, well educated, from a good family, with a better-than-average income. So, from now on, you're my favorite suitor."

"It's a great honor, señora."

"We have to make this girl come to her senses. She's not a bad person, you know, just strong willed. But then, she was so spoiled growing up. After that terrible catastrophe with my brother . . ."

"Catastrophe?" Augusto asked.

"Yes, and since it's public knowledge, there's no reason to hide it from you. Eugenia's father committed suicide after a disastrous stock-market venture, leaving her almost destitute. She inherited a house, but it's weighed down by a mortgage that consumes all her income. The poor girl is determined to save as much as she can to pay it off. Imagine, even if she were to give piano lessons for the next sixty years . . ."

Augusto immediately thought of a generous and heroic act.

"She's not a bad person, but she is hard to understand."

"If you learned Esperanto . . ." Don Fermín said.

"Forget about universal languages. We barely understand one another in our own language and you want to add another?"

"Don't you think it would be a good idea to have only one language?" Augusto asked.

"Exactly!" said Don Fermín, delighted.

"Yes, señor," the aunt said, "one language, Spanish, and, at the most, *bable* to speak to the maids, who have no common sense."

Eugenia's aunt was from Asturias, as was her maid, whom she scolded in *bable*.

"Now, if we're just speaking theoretically," she said, "I don't think it's a bad idea to have only one language. Because my husband here, in theory, is even opposed to matrimony."

"I'm afraid I may be disturbing you," Augusto said, rising.

"You can never disturb us, señor," the aunt said, "and you have to come again. You're now my favorite suitor, you know."

As Augusto was leaving, Don Fermín approached him and whispered in his ear, "Forget about all that."

"Why?" Augusto said.

"Premonitions, señor, premonitions," the uncle replied.

The aunt's last words to Augusto were, "Remember, you're my favorite suitor," and her first words to Eugenia when she came home were, "Do you know who's been here, Eugenia? Don Augusto Pérez."

"Augusto Pérez, Augusto Pérez? Oh, yes. Who brought him here?"

"My canary, Pichín."

"Why did he come?"

"Silly girl. Looking for you."

"For me? Brought by your canary? I don't understand. You may as well be speaking Esperanto, like Uncle Fermín."

"He was looking for you. He's a young man, not bad-looking, rather handsome, well-mannered, refined, and above all rich, child. He's rich."

"Well, he can keep his money. I'm not working this hard to sell myself."

"Who said anything about selling yourself? You're so prickly."

"All right, *tía*, that's enough. Let's drop this nonsense."

"You'll see for yourself, young lady. You'll see him and change your mind."

"As far as changing my mind . . ."

"No one can ever say, 'I'll never drink from this river,' " the aunt said.

"Mysterious are the ways of Providence!" Don Fermín declared. "God . . ."

"Oh, please," interrupted his wife, "how is God compatible with anarchism? I've asked you a thousand times. If no one's in charge, how does God fit into the picture?"

"As you've heard me say a thousand times, woman, my anarchism is mystical. It's a mystical anarchism. God doesn't command the way men do. God is also an anarchist. God doesn't command, He . . ."

"Obeys, is that it?"

"You said it, dear, you said it! God himself has enlightened you. Come here."

He held his wife, gazed at her forehead, blew softly on the curls of her white hair, and said, "He himself has inspired you. Yes, God obeys, He obeys."

"In theory, right? And you, Eugenia, don't be ridiculous, this is a great match for you."

"I'm an anarchist too, *tía*, but not like Uncle Fermín, not a mystical one."

"We'll see about that," her aunt said.

VII

"Oh, Orfeo!" Augusto was home, talking to Orfeo while feeding him his milk. "Oh, Orfeo! I've taken a big step, the decisive one. I went into her home, I entered the sanctuary. Do you know what it is to take a decisive step? The winds of fortune push us forward and our steps are decisive. *Our* steps? Are these steps really ours? We walk, Orfeo, through a wild, tangled forest without any trails. We create pathways with our feet as we proceed randomly. Some people believe they're following a star. I believe I'm following a double star, a twin star. That star is the projection of the pathway to the heavens, the projection of chance.

"A decisive step. Tell me, Orfeo, is it necessary for God or the world or anything to exist? Why must anything exist? Don't you think the idea of necessity might be the highest form chance takes in our minds?

"Where did Eugenia spring from? Is she my creation, or am I hers? Or are we two mutual creations, she mine and I hers? Maybe the whole is a creation of each individual thing and each individual thing a creation of the whole? What is creation anyway? What are you, Orfeo? What am I?

"I've often thought that I don't exist, Orfeo. I'd walk along the street imagining that other people couldn't see me. Other times I've fantasized that others didn't see me the way I saw myself, and that even though I thought I was walking normally, totally composed, I was acting crazily, and others were laughing and making fun of me. Has this ever happened to you, Orfeo? Probably not, because you're still young and have so little life experience. Besides, you're a dog. But tell me, Orfeo, do you think dogs will ever think they're men the way some men have thought they were dogs?

"What a life, Orfeo, especially since my mother died. Every hour of my life is driven by the hours preceding it. I've never known what the future looks like. And now that I begin to catch glimpses of it, I think it's going to turn into the past. Eugenia herself is almost a memory for me. These passing days . . . This day, this endless day that is passing, slipping by in a fog of boredom . . . Today like yesterday, tomorrow like today. Look, Orfeo. Look at the ashes my father left in that ashtray.

"This is the revelation of eternity, Orfeo, of terrible eternity. When man is left alone and closes his eyes to the future, to illusion, he perceives eternity's terrifying abyss. Eternity is not the future. When we die, death reverses our orbit and we begin to march backward, toward the past, toward what was. And so we proceed endlessly, unraveling our destiny's skein, undoing the infinity that took an eternity to create us, heading toward nothingness without ever reaching it, because it never was.

"Beneath this current of our existence, and within it, there's another current flowing in the opposite direction. In this life, we proceed from yesterday to tomorrow. In the countercurrent, we move from tomorrow to yesterday. We weave and unweave at the same time. And occasionally we perceive light breezes, vapors, and even mysterious murmurs from that other world, the world inside our world. History's innermost recesses contain a counterhistory inverting its course. The underground river flows from the sea back to its source.

"Eugenia's two eyes now shine in the heaven of my solitude. They shine with the iridescence of my mother's tears. And they make me believe I exist. Sweet illusion. *Amo, ergo sum!* This love, Orfeo, is like a merciful rain that both dissolves and condenses the fog of existence. Thanks to love, I can feel my soul in a palpable way, I can touch it. The very core of my soul aches, thanks to love. And what is the soul if not love, if not the incarnation of pain?

"Days come and go and love remains. Deep within, in the innermost depths, this world's current rubs and grates against the other world's current, and from this rubbing and grating comes the saddest and sweetest heartache of all, the heartache of living.

"Look at the threads, Orfeo, look at the warp. See how the shuttle contains the yarn. Watch the treadles bob up and down. Tell me, where is the warp beam on which we roll the fabric of our existence? Where?"

Since Orfeo had never seen a loom, he probably didn't comprehend his master. But gazing into Augusto's eyes as he spoke, he understood what he meant.

VIII

Augusto was shaking. As he sat there, he felt as if he were being stretched on a rack. He was aching to stand, pace around the room, shake his fists in the air, scream, act like a clown, forget he existed. Neither Doña Ermelinda, Eugenia's aunt, nor her husband, Don Fermín, the mystical, theoretical anarchist, were able to bring him down to earth.

"I think," Doña Ermelinda said, "that you should wait, Don Augusto. She shouldn't be long. Then you can meet and get acquainted, and that's the first step. These kinds of relationships have to begin with getting acquainted, don't you think?"

"Of course, señora," Augusto said, as if he were speaking from another world. "The first step is to meet and get acquainted."

"I think that as soon as she gets to know you . . . well, the rest is clear."

"Not that clear," Don Fermín said. "The ways of Providence are always mysterious. As for the idea that in order to marry it's necessary or even advisable to know each other, I disagree. The only effective knowledge comes *post nuptias*. You've heard me explain, my dear, what *knowing* signifies in the biblical sense. Believe me, there is no knowledge more essential and substantial than that, no knowledge more penetrating . . ."

"Hush, dear, hush. Don't be ridiculous."

"Knowledge, Ermelinda . . ."

The doorbell rang.

"That's her," the uncle said, in a mysterious voice.

Augusto felt a wave of fire rise from the floor and surge upward through his body and head and then disappear into the air above him. His heart began to pound. They heard the front door open and then quick, even, rhythmical steps, and Augusto, without knowing why, felt himself growing calm again.

"I'm going to call her," Don Fermín said, beginning to rise from his chair.

"Absolutely not," said Doña Ermelinda, summoning the maid.

When the maid appeared, the aunt said, "Ask señorita Eugenia to come here."

The three of them sat in silence, like conspirators, none of them speaking. Will I be able to bear it? Augusto thought. I might turn red as a poppy or white as a lily when her eyes appear in that doorway. My heart might burst.

They heard a soft rustle, like a dove taking flight, a brief and curt "Ah!" and Eugenia's eyes in a fresh, animated face, above a seemingly weightless body, shed a new mysterious spiritual light on the scene. Augusto felt calm, deeply calm—rooted to his chair as if he were a plant that had grown there—as if he were a vegetable. He was unselfconscious, absorbed in the mysterious spiritual light radiating from those eyes. Only when he heard Doña Ermelinda say, "This is our dear friend, Don Augusto Pérez," did he become aware of his surroundings again and stand, attempting to smile.

"This is our friend Don Augusto Pérez, who wanted to meet you."

"The canary man?"

"Yes, the canary man," Augusto said, approaching her, extending his hand. She's going to burn me with hers, he thought. But he was wrong. A cold white hand touched his, a hand as cold and white as snow, and Augusto felt a kind of liquid serenity flow through his body.

Eugenia sat down.

"And this gentleman . . ." said the pianist.

"This gentleman . . . this gentleman . . ." The phrase flashed through Augusto's mind. "This gentleman." Her calling me a gentleman is a bad sign, he thought.

"This gentleman, dear, who because of a timely coincidence . . ."

"Yes, the canary."

"Mysterious are the ways of Providence," the anarchist remarked.

"This gentleman," the aunt continued, "who, because of a timely coincidence, has made our acquaintance—and turns out to be the son of a lady whom I knew briefly and respected greatly—this gentleman, now a friend, wanted to meet you, Eugenia."

"And express his admiration," said Augusto.

"Admiration?" Eugenia said.

"Yes, for you as a pianist."

"Oh, my."

"I know your great love of art."

"What art? Music?"

"Of course."

"Then you've been deceived, Don Augusto."

Don Augusto? Don Augusto?, he thought. This "Don" is a bad omen, almost as bad as that "gentleman."

"Don't you like music?" he asked.

"Not at all, I swear."

Liduvina is right, he thought. After she's married, if her husband can support her, she'll never lay hands on a piano again.

"You have the reputation of being an excellent teacher," he said.

"I try to fulfill my professional obligations as best I can, and since I have to earn a living . . ."

"As far as having to earn a living . . ." Don Fermín said.

"Quiet," said the aunt. "Don Augusto has been informed of everything."

"Everything? What, exactly?" Eugenia began to get up from her chair.

"About the mortgage."

"What!" The niece stood up. "What is this about? What does all of this mean? Why did you come here?"

"I've already told you, dear, that this man wanted to meet you. Calm down."

"But there are some things that . . ."

"Please excuse your aunt," Augusto said, getting up from his chair, as did Eugenia's uncle and aunt. "I only wanted to meet you. As far as the mortgage and your sacrifice and the passion you have for your work, I didn't pry this interesting information from your aunt. I—"

"Right. All you did was return the canary a few days after sending me a letter."

"That's true, I don't deny it."

"Well, then, señor, I'll respond to that letter if and when I feel like it, without anyone pressuring me into doing it. And now I'd better say good-bye."

"Fantastic!" said Don Fermín. "This is integrity and freedom. This is the woman of the future. Women like this have to be won over forcefully, my dear Pérez."

"But, señorita . . ." Augusto walked toward her.

"Of course," Eugenia said, ending the visit by extending her hand, still as white and cold as snow. As she turned to leave, and as those eyes, the source of the mysterious spiritual light, were about to disappear, Augusto felt a wave of fire surge through his body again. He could feel his heart beating and his head seemed about to burst.

"Are you all right?" Don Fermín asked.

"That girl! Dear God, that girl!" said Doña Ermelinda.

"Incredible, majestic, heroic. A woman, quite a woman," Augusto said.

"I agree," the uncle said.

"Forgive her, Don Augusto," said the aunt, "forgive her. She is as prickly as a porcupine. Who would have thought?"

"But I find her delightful, señora, absolutely delightful. Her fierce independence, which I lack, is what I like most about her. This, this and no other, is the woman I need."

"Yes, señor Pérez," the anarchist said. "This is the woman of the future."

"What about me?" said Doña Ermelinda.

"You're the woman of the past. She, I say, is the woman of the future. Of course, she's heard me speak day after day about the society and women of the future. My efforts to instill in her the emancipating doctrines of anarchism—without bombs, of course—have not been in vain."

"Well, I think this girl is quite capable of throwing bombs," the aunt said.

"Even if that were true . . ." Augusto said.

"Never! Never!" said the uncle.

"What difference does it make?"

"Don Augusto! Don Augusto!"

"I don't think you should be discouraged by what happened," the aunt said.

"Of course not. This makes her even more worthwhile."

"Court her, then. You know we're on your side. You can come here anytime you want, whether Eugenia likes it or not."

"She hasn't said that Don Augusto's visits displease her," the uncle said. "But you'll have to win her over forcefully, my friend, forcefully. You'll get to know her and see what she's made of. She's quite a woman, Don Augusto, and you have to conquer her forcefully. You said you wanted to get to know her."

"Yes, but . . ."

"Then that's that. Into the breach, my friend!"

"Of course, of course, and now good-bye."

Don Fermín took Augusto aside and said, "I forgot to mention that when you write to Eugenia, you should write her name with a *j* instead of a *g*: Eujenia, and del Arco with a *k*: Eujenia Domingo del Arko."

"But why?"

"Because, until that happy day when Esperanto is the only language—one language for all humanity—we must write Spanish phonetically. No more *c*'s. Down with the *c*! *Za, ze, zi, zo, zu* with a *z*, and *ka, ke, ki, ko, ku* with a *k*. And down with the *h*. The *h* is absurd, reactionary, authoritarian, medieval, and backward. Down with the *h*!"

"You're also a phonetician?"

"Also? Why also?"

"Because you're an anarchist and Esperantist."

"It's all the same, señor, all one and the same. Anarchism, Esperantism, spiritism, vegetarianism, phoneticism—it's all one. Down with authority. Down with different languages. Down with vile matter and death. Down with the flesh. Down with the *h*! Good day."

They said good-bye, and Augusto left the house feeling that a weight had been lifted from his shoulders, even joyful. He would never have anticipated feeling so good. Eugenia's manner the first time they met and talked hadn't disturbed him. Instead, it energized him and spurred him on. The world seemed larger, the air purer, the sky bluer. It was as if he were breathing for the first time. Deep inside he could hear his mother's words: "Get married!" Almost all the women he passed on the street seemed pretty, many of them beautiful, not a single one of them ugly. It seemed that a new, mysterious light was beginning to illuminate the world, a light emanating from two large invisible stars shimmering beyond the blue of the sky, beyond heaven's dome. He was beginning to get to know the world. Without knowing why, he began to think about the profound reasons people commonly associate the sins of the flesh with the fall of our first parents after they ate from the tree of the knowledge of good and evil. And he pondered Don Fermín's doctrine regarding the origin of knowledge.

He arrived home and when Orfeo scampered out to greet him, he scooped the dog up in his arms, patted him, and said, "Today we begin a new life, Orfeo. Don't you feel that the world is bigger, the air purer, the sky bluer? Ah, when you see her, Orfeo, when you get to know her . . . Then you'll feel the anguish of being only a dog as I feel the anguish of being only a man. Tell me, Orfeo, how do dogs ever know anything if they haven't sinned? Knowledge that isn't a sin isn't real knowledge, it's not rational."

When his faithful Liduvina served him lunch, she stood there, staring at him.

"What are you looking at?" Augusto said.

"You've changed."

"How?"

"Your face looks different."

"You think so?"

"Of course. Are things working out with the piano teacher?"

"Liduvina! Liduvina!"

"You're right, señor, I'm just concerned about your happiness."

"Who knows what that is?"

"True."

The two of them looked down at the floor, as if the secret to happiness lay beneath it.

IX

The next day Eugenia was chatting with a young man in the small lobby of a nearby apartment building. The concierge had discreetly left to get some air outside the front door.

"This has to stop, Mauricio," Eugenia said. "We can't go on like this, especially after what I told you happened yesterday."

"Didn't you say this suitor is a poor sap with his head in the clouds?" Mauricio said.

"Yes, but he has money, and my aunt isn't going to leave me alone. Honestly, I don't like to be rude, but I don't want anyone pestering me either."

"Get rid of him."

"Tell him not to come to my aunt and uncle's house? What if they insist?"

"Then ignore him."

"I do and I will, but I have a hunch the poor guy is going to come over whenever I'm home. There's no point in shutting myself up in my room and refusing to see him. He'll become a silent martyr."

"Let him."

"No, I can't resist beggars, especially the ones who plead with their eyes. You should see the looks he gives me."

"Do you pity him?"

"I find him annoying. But the truth is . . . why shouldn't I tell you? Yes, I pity him."

"Are you afraid?"

"Don't be silly. I'm not afraid of anything. I'm not interested in anyone but you."

"I knew it," Mauricio said. He put his hand on Eugenia's knee.

"You have to make up your mind, Mauricio."

"About what, gorgeous?"

"What do you think? About getting married once and for all."

"What are we going to live on?"

"On my income, until you find a job."

"On your income?"

"Yes, on that hateful music."

"On your income? Impossible. Never. I would rather do anything than live off your piano lessons. I'll look, I'll keep looking, and in the meantime, we'll wait."

"We'll wait . . . we'll wait, and the years will slip away!" Eugenia said, stomping the floor with her foot, bouncing the leg where Mauricio's hand was resting.

Mauricio took his hand off Eugenia's knee. He put his arm around her neck and began to play with one of her earrings. She didn't pull away.

"Listen, Eugenia, if you want, you can toy with this fool."

"Mauricio!"

"You're right, don't get mad, baby." He drew Eugenia's head closer, moved toward her lips, closed his eyes, and gave her a long, wet, silent kiss.

"Mauricio!"

Then he kissed her eyes.

"We can't go on like this, Mauricio."

"Why not? Is there anything better than this? Do you think we'll ever have a better time than this?"

"I'm telling you, we can't go on like this. You have to get a job. I hate music."

Eugenia had a vague, semiconscious feeling that music was an endless preparation for an event that would never take place, an interminable beginning leading to nothing. She was sick of music.

"I'll look for work, Eugenia, I will."

"You always say that and then nothing happens."

"Do you think . . . ?"

"I know that down deep you're lazy and that I'll have to find you a job. It's so much easier for men to wait."

"That's what you think."

"I know what I'm talking about, and I'm telling you again, I don't want to see Don Augusto's pleading eyes. They remind me of a starving puppy."

"What a thing to say!"

"And now," she said, standing and pushing him away, "be a good boy and get some fresh air. You need it badly."

"Eugenia! Eugenia!" he whispered in her ear in a parched, almost feverish voice. "If you loved . . ."

"You're the one who needs to learn how to love, Mauricio. Be a man. Look for a job and make up your mind soon. If not, I'll keep teaching. But make up your mind soon. Otherwise . . ."

"Otherwise, what?"

"Nothing. We just can't go on like this."

Without giving him a chance to reply, she left the reception area. As she passed the concierge, she said, "Your nephew is still in there, señora Marta. Tell him to make up his mind once and for all."

Eugenia went out onto the street with her head held high. Just then an organ-grinder began to play a furious polka. "Horrible! Horrible!" she said to herself, and fled down the street.

X

Augusto needed to confide in someone, so the day after his visit to Eugenia's house, while she was spurring her boyfriend to action, he walked to the club to see his good friend Victor.

He felt like a different man. It was as if his visit and the revelation that she was a tough woman—her eyes shone with strength—had plowed the depths of his soul and uncovered a hidden spring. He walked more resolutely, breathed more freely.

Now I have a goal, a purpose in life, he thought. To conquer this girl or be conquered by her. There's no difference. In love there's no difference between conquering and being conquered. Although . . . No, in this case, if she prevails, she leaves me for the other guy. Yes, I'm sure there's another. Another? Another what? Am I even one of them? I'm an admirer, a suitor, but the other . . . I get the feeling that the other guy is not an admirer or a suitor because he's already gotten what he wants, nothing more than Eugenia's love. Nothing more?

A female body passing by, glowing with freshness, health, and happiness, interrupted his thoughts and dragged him along. He followed her, almost reflexively, while continuing his soliloquy.

This one's stunning, he thought. This one and that one, all of them. Maybe this other guy, instead of wooing and chasing is wooed and chased. Maybe he doesn't treat her the way she deserves. This girl is pure joy. Look how adorably she greets that man over there. Where did she get those eyes? They look like Eugenia's. How sweet it must be to forget life and death in those arms. To be rocked in them as if they were gentle waves of flesh. The other . . . The other isn't Eugenia's boyfriend. He's not the man she loves. I'm the other. Yes, I'm the other. I'm another.

As he reached the conclusion that he was another, the young woman he was following entered a doorway. Augusto stopped and gazed at the house. That's when he realized he'd been following her. He remembered that he'd been heading to the club and turned in that direction.

My God, there are so many beautiful women in the world, he thought. Almost all of them are beautiful. Thank you, Lord, thank you. *Gratias agimus tibi propter magnam gloriam tuam!* Your glory, Lord, is reflected in women's beauty. What hair, dear God, what hair!

The servant girl who passed him with a basket on her arm did indeed have glorious hair. He turned to follow her. The light seemed to nestle in the golden strands of her hair, which looked as if they were struggling to break free from her braids and scatter in the cool, clear air. Her face beamed from beneath her golden mane.

I am other, I'm the other, Augusto thought as he followed the girl with the basket. Are there no other women? Yes, for the other guy. But like her, like the one and only? No one. None. These others are mere copies of her—of the one, the only—my sweet Eugenia.

Mine? Of course, with my thoughts and desires, I make her mine. He, the other guy, may possess her physically, but the mysterious spiritual light of those eyes is mine, all mine. But doesn't this golden hair also reflect a mysterious spiritual light? And is there only one Eugenia or are there two, mine and her fiancé's? If there are two, let him keep his and I'll keep mine. When I feel sad, especially at night—when I feel like crying for no reason at all—how sweet it'll be to cover my face, my mouth, and my eyes with this golden hair and to breathe the air that it filters and perfumes. But—

His reflections were suddenly cut short. The girl with the basket had stopped to talk to a friend. Augusto hesitated for a moment. Never mind, he thought, there are so many beautiful women since I met Eugenia . . . He continued his walk, turning toward the club.

If she insists on choosing the other guy, he thought, I'm capable of making a heroic decision, something shockingly magnanimous. After all, whether she loves me or not, something has to be done about the mortgage.

He was startled out of his soliloquy by a burst of glee that seemed to erupt from the clear blue sky. Two girls were laughing nearby, and their laughter sounded like birds chirping deep within a flowering bush. He stared at the girls with eyes thirsting for beauty. They looked like they were fused together, walking arm in arm. He felt a wild impulse to stop them, stand between them, take each one by the arm, and walk with them—gazing up at the sky—wherever the winds of life might take them.

There've been so many beautiful women since I met Eugenia, he thought, as he followed the laughing girls. This is heaven. What eyes, what hair, what laughter! One is blond and the other brunette, but which is the blond and which is the brunette? I can't tell them apart.

"Hey, there! Are you awake or asleep, Augusto?"

"Hello, Victor."

"I waited for you at the club, but when you didn't show up . . ."

"I was on my way."

"On your way? Heading in this direction? Have you lost your mind?"

"You're right. Look, I'll tell you the truth. I think I told you about Eugenia."

"The pianist? Yes."

"I'm madly in love with her, like a . . ."

"Like a man in love. Go on."

"Madly, my friend, madly. Yesterday I saw her in her home with the excuse of visiting her aunt and uncle. I saw her—"

"And she looked at you, right? And you believed in God?"

"No, she didn't look at me. She enveloped me in her gaze. And I didn't believe in God, I believed that I *was* a god."

"You've got it bad."

"Yes, even though she was testy. I don't know what's happened to me since. Nearly all the women I see look beautiful, and since I left my house barely half an hour ago, I've already fallen in love with three—no, four. The first one was all eyes, another had a glorious head of hair, and just now, there was a pair, a blond and a brunette, who laughed like angels. And I followed all four. What's happening to me?"

"What's happening, Augusto, is that your reservoir of love was lying dormant at the bottom of your soul with nowhere to flow. Eugenia the piano teacher came along. She shook you up, and her eyes stirred up the pool where all that love was sleeping. It awoke and is so plentiful that it's overflowing in all directions. When a man like you really falls in love with one woman, he falls in love with all women."

"I thought it would be just the opposite. By the way, look at that brunette. She is luminous night. They're right when they say that black absorbs more light than any other color. Can't you feel the light hidden beneath her hair, behind those jet-black eyes? Let's follow her."

"If you want."

"I thought it would be just the opposite. That when a man truly falls in love, instead of his love spilling over onto all women, it would be focused only on one, and the rest would be reduced to nothing and lose all value. Look how the sun glistens on her black hair."

"No, let's see if I can explain it to you. You were in love, unknowingly of course, with woman in the abstract, not with this one or that one in particular. When you saw Eugenia, that abstraction became concrete. Woman became one woman, and you fell in love with her. Now you're branching out, without abandoning her, to all the others. You're falling in love with women collectively, with the gender. You've moved from the abstract to the concrete, and from the concrete to the generic—from Woman to one woman, and from one woman to women."

"Now you're getting metaphysical."

"What is love if not metaphysics?"

"Oh, please!"

"Especially in your case. Your falling in love is purely cerebral. It's all in your head."

"That's what you think," Augusto said, a bit annoyed and ill-tempered. The suggestion that his falling in love was only in his head hurt him to the depths of his soul.

"In fact, if you push me, I'll tell you that you yourself are nothing but an idea, a fictional character."

"You think I'm incapable of really falling in love like everyone else?"

"I'm sure you're really in love, but only in your head. You think you're in love."

"Is there more to being in love than thinking that you are?"

"Good grief, that's more complicated than you can possibly imagine."

"Tell me, how do you know you're really in love and not just that you think you are?"

"Look, we'd better change the subject and talk about something else."

When Augusto returned home, he picked up Orfeo and said, "Let's see, Orfeo, how is being in love different from just thinking that you are? Am I or aren't I in love with Eugenia? Doesn't my heart pound in my chest and my blood feel like it's on fire when I see her? Aren't I like other men? I have to prove that I'm just like them, Orfeo."

At suppertime he went up to Liduvina and asked, "How can you tell if a man is really in love, Liduvina?"

"You ask such strange questions, señor."

"So, how can you tell?"

"Well, you know it when he says and does a lot of stupid things. When a man really falls in love with a woman . . . let's say he's crazy about a woman, he stops being a man."

"What is he then?"

"He's . . . he's . . . he's a thing, like a small animal. A woman can do whatever she wants with him."

"So when a woman truly falls in love with a man, when she's crazy about a man, as you say, can the man do whatever he wants with her?"

"It's not the same."

"Why not?"

"It's hard to explain, señor. Are you really in love?"

"That's what I'm trying to find out. But I don't think I've said or done anything really stupid yet."

Liduvina was silent, and Augusto wondered, Am I really in love?

XI

When Augusto returned the next day to Don Fermín and Doña Ermelinda's house, the maid showed him into the drawing room and said, "I'll let them know you're here." He was alone for a few minutes, as if in a vacuum. There was a tightness deep in his chest, and he was overwhelmed by an agonizing feeling of solemnity. He sat down, then quickly stood up again and passed the time examining the paintings on the wall, among them a portrait of Eugenia. He felt like running away, fleeing. Suddenly, when he heard light footsteps, he felt an icy dagger pierce his chest and a fog seep into his head. The door to the drawing room opened and Eugenia appeared. The poor man leaned on the back of an armchair. Seeing his ashen face, she grew pale herself for a moment and stood motionless in the middle of the room.

Then she came closer. In a quiet, curt voice she asked, "What's the matter, Don Augusto? Are you ill?"

"No, it's nothing. I don't know."

"Is there something I can get you? Do you need anything?"

"A glass of water."

Relieved to have something to do, Eugenia left the room and came back quickly. The water quivered in the glass, but it shook even more in Augusto's hands. He drank it in one gulp, clumsily, spilling water on his chin, his eyes glued to Eugenia's.

"If you want, I'll have them bring you a cup of tea—chamomile, or another herb tea. Are you feeling better?"

"No, no. It was nothing. Thank you, Eugenia, thank you," he said, drying his chin.

"Well then, please sit down." Once they were seated she said, "I was expecting you to come any day now and told the maid that even if my aunt and uncle were to go out in the afternoon, as they sometimes do, she should invite you in and inform me. I wanted to speak to you alone."

"Oh, Eugenia, Eugenia!"

"Let's take things calmly. I never imagined you'd get so carried away. You scared me when I saw you. You looked like a dead man."

"I was more dead than alive, believe me."

"We need to speak frankly."

"Eugenia!" the wretched man cried. He held out his hand only to pull it back quickly.

"I don't think you're quite ready to speak sensibly, like good friends. Let's see." She took his hand to feel his pulse.

Poor Augusto's pulse began to beat feverishly. He turned red, his forehead burned. His vision blurred, and he couldn't see Eugenia's eyes anymore, only a red fog. For a moment he thought he was going to faint.

"Have pity on me, Eugenia! Have pity!"

"Calm down, Don Augusto, calm down!"

"Don Augusto, Don Augusto, Don, Don . . ."

"Yes, Don Augusto, relax. Let's talk calmly."

"Let me . . ." He reached with both hands for her right hand, as cold and white as snow, with tapered fingers made to caress piano keys and pluck out sweet arpeggios.

"All right, Don Augusto."

He raised her hand to his lips and covered it with kisses, barely warming its pale coolness.

"When you've finished, Don Augusto, we'll start talking."

"Please, Eugenia, come—"

"No, behave yourself." She removed her hand and said, "I don't know what my aunt and uncle have led you to believe—especially my aunt—but I think they've misled you."

"Misled me, how?"

"They should have told you that I have a fiancé."

"I know that."

"Did they tell you?"

"No, no one told me, but I know."

"Well, then—"

"Honestly, I have no expectations, Eugenia. I'm not looking or asking for anything. I'll be satisfied if you allow me to come over once in a while to bathe my soul in the glances of your eyes and be transported by the vapors of your sweet breath."

"Those are things that we read in books, Don Augusto. Let's drop all that. I don't object to your coming over as often as you like and seeing me day in, day out. You may speak to me, you may even—as you've seen—you may even kiss my hand. But I have a fiancé whom I love and plan to marry."

"Are you really in love with him?"

"What kind of a question is that?"

"How do you know you're in love with him?"

"Have you lost your mind, Don Augusto?"

"No. I ask because my best friend told me that lots of people only think they're in love."

"He said that about you, didn't he?"

"Yes, he said that about me. Why?"

"In your case, it might be true."

"You don't think I'm really in love with you, Eugenia?"

"Keep your voice down, Don Augusto, the maid might hear you."

"Yes," he said, becoming more and more agitated. "Some people think I'm incapable of really falling in love."

"Excuse me a moment," Eugenia interrupted. She exited the room, leaving him alone.

She returned a short while later and asked coolly, "Have you calmed down now, Don Augusto?"

"Eugenia! Eugenia!"

They heard a knock at the door and Eugenia said, "My aunt and uncle!" A few moments later the elderly couple entered the room.

"Don Augusto came to see you. I opened the door myself. He wanted to leave, but I told him to come in, that you wouldn't be long. And here he is."

"There will come a time," Don Fermín said, "when all social conventions will vanish. I'm convinced that the fences and walls that surround private property are nothing but incitements for so-called thieves. The real thieves are the property owners. The safest properties don't have fences or walls and are open to everyone. Men are born good and are good by nature. Society corrupts and perverts them."

"Hush," Doña Ermelinda said. "I can't hear the canary sing. Can you hear it, Don Augusto? It's delightful to listen to. You should have heard the canary I had when Eugenia used to practice the piano. He would get so excited. The more she pounded the keys, the more he would sing. In the end it killed him, he burst . . ."

"Our vices even rub off on our pets," the uncle said. "We've uprooted the animals that live with us from their sacred natural environment. Oh, humanity!"

"Have you been waiting long, Don Augusto?" asked the aunt.

"Oh, no, señora, not long at all. A brief moment, a lightning flash. At least that's how it seemed to me."

"I see."

"Yes, *tía*, very little time. But long enough for him to recover from a slight ailment he brought in from the street."

"What do you mean?"

"It was nothing, señora."

"Well, I'll leave you now, I have things to do," Eugenia said. She shook Augusto's hand and left.

"How is it going?" the aunt asked Augusto, once Eugenia was out of the room.

"How's what going?"

"The conquest, of course."

"Very badly. She informed me that she has a fiancé and that she plans to marry him."

"Didn't I tell you, Ermelinda? Didn't I?" the uncle said.

"No. That's impossible. That fiancé is sheer madness, Don Augusto."

"But what if she's in love with him?"

"That's what I say!" the uncle exclaimed. "Freedom, sacred freedom, freedom of choice!"

"No, no, no. Do you think this girl knows what she's doing? Reject you, Don Augusto? You? That's unacceptable!"

"Stop for a moment and think, señora. No one should oppose the will of a young woman like Eugenia. Her happiness is at stake, and it's our duty to think only of that and even sacrifice ourselves for it."

"Sacrifice yourself, Don Augusto?"

"Yes, señora. I'm willing to sacrifice myself for Eugenia, your niece's, happiness, because my happiness depends on hers."

"Bravo!" the uncle said. "Bravo! Bravo! Behold a hero! Behold a mystical anarchist!"

"Anarchist?" Augusto said.

"Yes, anarchist. My anarchism consists precisely of this, that each of us sacrifice himself for others, that our happiness depend on making others happy, that—"

"Fermín, you have a fit if your soup is ten minutes late!" the aunt said.

"Well, as you know, my anarchism is theoretical, Ermelinda. I strive for perfection, but—"

"Happiness is also theoretical," Augusto muttered to himself gloomily. Then he declared, "I've decided to sacrifice myself for Eugenia's happiness, and I've thought of a heroic act."

"What is it?"

"Didn't you once tell me, señora, that the house Eugenia's unfortunate father left her . . ."

"Yes, my poor brother."

". . . has a mortgage that consumes all her income?"

"Yes, señor."

"Well, then, I know what I have to do." He moved toward the door.

"But Don Augusto . . ."

"Augusto feels capable of making the most heroic decisions and the greatest sacrifices. Now we'll see whether he loves only with his head or also with his heart, whether he's truly in love or only thinks that he is. Eugenia has awakened me to life—to real life. No matter who she belongs to, I owe her an eternal debt of gratitude. And now, good-bye."

He departed solemnly. He'd barely gone when he heard Doña Ermelinda shout, "Young lady!"

XII

"Señor," Liduvina said the next day to Augusto, "the girl who does the ironing is here."

"The girl who does the ironing? Oh, of course, show her in."

The young girl entered carrying a basket with Augusto's clothes. They looked at each other and the poor girl felt her cheeks turn red. In all the times she'd been to this house, nothing like this had ever happened to her. The gentleman had previously seemed unaware of her presence, something she'd found disconcerting and even annoying. She thought she knew her own worth. To ignore her, not to look at her the way other men did, not to devour her with his eyes and feast on her mouth, her eyes, her entire face . . .

"What's the matter, Rosario? That's your name, isn't it?"

"Yes, that's my name."

"What's the matter?"

"Why, señor Augusto?"

"I've never seen you blush like this, and you seem different."

"You're the one who seems different."

"Well, maybe. Come here, come closer."

"Stop joking and let's settle the bill."

"Joking? You think I'm joking?" he said in a more serious tone. "Come closer, let me get a good look at you."

"Haven't you seen me many times before?"

"Yes, but I never noticed how pretty you are."

"Please don't tease me," her face felt hot.

"Especially now, with your pink cheeks, glowing like the sun."

"Please."

"Come closer, come. You probably think that señor Augusto has lost his mind, don't you? But no, that's not it. The truth is that he's been crazy all along, or rather he's been a fool, a complete fool, lost in a fog, blind. My eyes were opened only a little while ago. You've been in this house many times and I've looked right at you but never seen you. It's as if I hadn't lived, Rosarito. I was a fool. What's the matter, sweetheart? What's wrong?"

Rosario had had to sit down. She hid her face in her hands and burst into tears. Augusto stood up, closed the door, walked back to the young woman, put his hand on her shoulder, and said quietly, in his warmest, kindest voice, "What's wrong? What is it, sweetheart?"

"When you speak to me like that, you make me cry, Don Augusto."

"You're an angel!"

"You shouldn't say such things, Don Augusto."

"What do you mean? I've lived my life blindly and foolishly. I was barely alive until a woman came into it, understand? Another woman. She opened my eyes, and I saw the world. Above all, I've learned to see you, all women—"

"That woman . . . she must be bad."

"You say she's bad? Do you know what you're saying, Rosario? Do you know what it means to be bad? What does it mean? No, no. That woman, like you, is an angel. But that woman doesn't love me, she doesn't love me." As he said this, his voice broke and his eyes filled with tears.

"Poor Don Augusto."

"You're right, Rosario. Poor Don Augusto. But listen, Rosario, forget the 'Don' and say, 'Poor Augusto.' Come on, say it. 'Poor Augusto.'"

"But, señor . . ."

"Come on, say it. 'Poor Augusto.'"

"If you insist. Poor Augusto."

Augusto sat down.

"Come here," he said.

She jumped to her feet, like someone obeying a hypnotic suggestion. She was breathing heavily. He reached out, sat her on his knees, and held her tightly against his chest. He pressed his cheek against her flushed face.

"Oh, Rosario," he said. "I don't know what's happening to me. I'm not myself. That woman you say is bad—even though you've never met her—blinded me when she gave me sight. I wasn't living and now I am. But now that I'm living, I feel what it's like to die. I have to protect myself from that woman, from her eyes. Will you help me, Rosario? Will you help protect me from her?"

A faint "yes," like a whisper from a distant world, brushed past Augusto's ear.

"I don't know what's happening to me anymore, Rosario. Not what I say, what I do, what I think. I don't even know if I'm in love with that woman you say is bad."

"Don Augusto, it's just that I—"

"Just Augusto, Augusto."

"Augusto, it's just that I—"

"All right, hush now, that's enough." He closed his eyes. "Don't say anything. Let me just talk to myself alone. That's how I've lived since my mother died—alone, completely alone. In other words, asleep. I haven't known what it's like to sleep with someone and share the same dream. To sleep together. Not to be together, each dreaming his own dream . . . No, to sleep together sharing the same dream. What if you and I shared the same dream, Rosario?"

"But that woman . . ." said the poor girl, trembling in Augusto's arms, her voice filled with tears.

"That woman, Rosario, doesn't love me. She doesn't love me. But she's shown me that other women exist. Because of her I've learned that there are other women, and one of them will be able to love me. Will you love me, Rosario? Tell me, will you love me?" He clasped her to his chest.

"I think so. I think that I'll love you, señor."

"Just 'you,' Rosario, 'that I'll love *you*.'"

"That I'll love you."

"That's it, Rosario. Hey!"

Just then the door opened and Liduvina appeared. She exclaimed "Oh!" and immediately closed it again. Augusto was much more flustered than Rosario, who stood up quickly, smoothed her hair, and said, "Shall we settle the bill, señor?"

"Yes, of course. But you'll come back, won't you?"

"Yes, I'll come back."

"And you forgive me for everything? Do you forgive me?"

"Forgive you? For what?"

"For this. I lost my mind for a moment. Will you forgive me?"

"There's nothing to forgive, señor. You need to stop thinking about that woman."

"What about you? Will you think about me?"

"Please. I've got to go."

He paid the bill and Rosario left. She was barely gone when Liduvina came into the room.

"Didn't you ask me the other day how to tell if a man is really in love?"

"I did."

"And I said it's when he says or does crazy things. Well, I can assure you now that you're really in love."

"But with whom? With Rosario?"

"Rosario? Of course not. With the other one."

"What gave you that idea, Liduvina?"

"Well, you've been saying and doing things to this girl that you couldn't say or do to the other one."

"You don't think . . . ?"

"No. I'm sure you haven't gone too far, but—"

"Liduvina! Liduvina!"

"Whatever you say, señor."

The poor man went to lie down, his head burning. Orfeo was sleeping at the foot of his bed. As he lay down he thought, Oh, Orfeo, this business of sleeping alone, all alone, dreaming one dream alone . . . The dream of one person is an illusion, an appearance. The dream of two people is truth, reality. What is the real world but a dream that we all dream, a shared dream?

And he fell into a dream.

XIII

One morning a few days later, Liduvina entered Augusto's bedroom and told him that a young lady was asking to see him.

"A young lady?"

"Yes, the piano teacher."

"Eugenia?"

"Yes, Eugenia. Obviously you're not the only one who's lost his mind."

Poor Augusto began to shake. He felt like a criminal. He got out of bed, washed quickly, got dressed, and came out prepared for anything.

"I've learned, Don Augusto, that you've settled my debt," Eugenia said solemnly as soon as he appeared, "and that you now own the mortgage on my house."

"It's true."

"What right did you have to do this?"

"The right, señorita, that any citizen has to buy whatever he wants if the owner is willing to sell it."

"That's not what I mean. I mean why did you buy it?"

"Because it pained me to see you so dependent on a man who probably couldn't care less about you and who I suspect is a heartless speculator."

"In other words, you would rather have me be dependent on you because you have feelings for me."

"Never! Never, Eugenia, never! I don't want to make you dependent on me. The mere thought of it is offensive. You'll see." He left the room, agitated.

He returned a short while later holding some papers.

"Here are the documents securing your debt, Eugenia. Take them and do whatever you want with them."

"What?"

"I want nothing to do with it. That's why I paid it off."

"I knew it. And that's why I said you want to make me dependent on you. You want my gratitude to bind me to you. You want to buy me!"

"Eugenia!"

"You want to buy me! That's what you want. You want to buy . . . not my love, that can't be bought, but my body!"

"Eugenia!"

"Whether you believe it or not, that's shameful, downright shameful!"

"Eugenia, for heaven's sake!"

"Don't come any closer. I don't know what I might do."

"I will come closer. Hit me, Eugenia, hit me! Insult me, spit on me, do whatever you want with me!"

"You deserve nothing." Eugenia stood up. "I'm leaving, but understand that I will not accept your charity or your offer. I'll work harder than ever. I'll make my fiancé, who'll soon be my husband, get a job, and we'll go on with our lives. As far as the house is concerned, keep it."

"I'm not opposed to you marrying this fiancé of yours, Eugenia."

"What? What do you mean? Tell me."

"I didn't do this so that you'd marry me out of gratitude. I renounce my own happiness. I mean, my happiness consists of your being happy with the man you choose to be your husband."

"Oh, now I understand. You're going to play the heroic victim, the martyr. I'm telling you to keep the house. It's a gift from me to you."

"But Eugenia, Eugenia . . ."

"Enough!"

Without another look, those two blazing eyes disappeared. For a moment, Augusto was beside himself, unaware of his own existence. Once he shook off the fog of confusion surrounding him, he got his hat, rushed out onto the street, and began to wander aimlessly. When he came to the church of San Martín, he entered, barely aware of what he was doing. He could see only the faint glow of the lamp before the main altar. He seemed to be inhaling darkness, the scent of antiquity, of tradition steeped in incense, and of a centuries-old home. He groped his way almost blindly to a pew and sat down. Actually, he collapsed onto it. He was mortally exhausted, as if all the darkness and antiquity he was inhaling weighed heavily on his heart. Now and then he heard a distant murmur, a very distant murmur, giving rise to a short cough. He remembered his mother.

Augusto closed his eyes and dreamed once again of that sweet, warm house where the light streamed through the white flowers embroidered on the curtains. He saw his mother again, coming and going silently with a tearful smile, always dressed in black. And he recalled his life as her son, when they were inseparable and she protected him. Then the poor woman's slow, grave, gentle, and painless death, when she departed like a migrating bird, silently taking flight. Next he remembered, or redreamed, finding Orfeo. A short while later, his emotional state was such that it caused strange, cinematic images to appear in his mind.

A man sitting nearby was whispering his prayers. He stood up to leave and Augusto followed him. At the church's entrance, the man dipped the first and second fingers of his right hand into the font and then offered the holy water to Augusto before crossing himself. They met again at the gate.

"Don Avito!" Augusto exclaimed.

"Yes, it's me, Augustito."

"You? Here?"

"Yes. Life teaches us many things and death teaches us even more. They teach us much more than science."

"How's the budding genius?"

Don Avito Carrascal told him the tragic story of his son. He concluded by saying, "So you see, Augustito, how I've come to this."

Augusto stared at the ground quietly. They were walking along the Alameda.

"Yes, Augusto," Don Avito continued. "Only life teaches us about life. Pedagogy is useless. You learn to live only by living, and each person has to begin from the beginning."

"What about the work of previous generations, Don Avito? The legacy passed down through the ages?"

"Only two legacies are passed down through the ages: illusions and disappointments, both of which are found exactly where we ran into each other a little while ago—in church. You probably ended up there because of a great illusion or a great disappointment."

"Both, actually."

"Both, yes. Because illusion and hope breed disappointment and memories, and disappointment and memories, in turn, breed illusion and hope. Science deals with reality, my friend, with the present, and I can no longer live in the present. Ever since Apolodoro, my poor victim, died," his voice choked with grief, "or rather, killed himself, I can't live in the present. Science and reality mean nothing to me. I can't live without remembering him or hoping to see him again. So I go to church, the place that harbors all illusions and disappointments."

"You're a believer now?"

"Who knows?"

"You're not a believer?"

"I don't know whether I am or not. I know that I pray, but I'm not sure what my prayers are about. A few of us gather there to say the rosary. I don't know who they are, and they don't know me, but we feel a sense of solidarity, an intimate connection to one another. And I now think that humanity has no damn need of geniuses."

"How's your wife, Don Avito?"

"Ah, my wife," said Carrascal. A tear that had appeared in one of his eyes seemed to shine with an inner light. "My wife . . . I've discovered her. Until the unspeakable tragedy occurred, I didn't know how special she was. I was able to penetrate life's mystery only when, in the terrible nights following my Apolodoro's suicide, I rested my head in his mother's lap and cried and cried. She stroked my head softly, saying, 'My poor son! My poor son!' Never has she been more of a mother than she is now. When I made her a mother—so that she could provide me with the raw material for a genius—I never thought that one day I would need her as a mother myself. I never knew my own mother, Augusto. I never knew what it was like to have a mother until my wife and I lost our son, and my wife became like a mother to me. You knew your mother, Augusto, the wonderful Doña Soledad. Otherwise, I'd advise you to get married."

"I knew her, Don Avito, but I lost her. I was thinking of her just now in the church."

"If you want to get your mother back, get married, Augusto."

"No. I'll never get my mother back."

"That's true, but get married anyway."

"How?" Augusto said, with a sly smile, recalling what he'd heard about one of Don Avito's theories. "How? Deductively or inductively?"

"Forget about all of that now. For God's sake, Augusto, don't remind me of tragic events. But . . . well, all right, let's keep the joke going and say marry intuitively."

"What if the woman I love doesn't love me back?"

"Marry a woman who loves you, even if you don't love her. It's better if she has to win you over than the other way around. Find one who loves you."

The image of the girl who did the ironing flashed through Augusto's mind. He'd deluded himself into thinking the poor girl was in love with him.

When Augusto finally said good-bye to Don Avito, he headed toward the club. He wanted to clear the fog in his head and his heart by playing a game of chess with Victor.

XIV

Augusto noticed that his friend Victor was acting strangely. He was playing badly and was silent and irritable.

"Victor, something's wrong."

"You're right. Something serious has happened to me. I need to get it off my chest. Let's go outside. It's a beautiful evening and I'll tell you all about it."

Although Victor was Augusto's closest friend, he was five or six years older and had been married for more than twelve years. He'd married very young, to do the honorable thing, people said. He had no children.

Out on the street, Victor remarked, "Augusto, you know that I had to get married when I was very young."

"You had to get married?"

"Don't pretend you didn't know. Everyone's heard the rumors. My parents and Elena's parents forced us to get married when we were kids. Marriage was a game for us. We played at being husband and wife. But it turned out to be a false alarm."

"What turned out to be a false alarm?"

"The reason they made us get married. Our parents' prudishness. They learned of a small misstep on our part, which caused a bit of a scandal, and rather than wait and see what the consequences were—or if there would be any—they made us get married."

"They were right."

"I'm not so sure. In any case, that small misstep had no consequences, and neither did any of the other missteps after we were married."

"Missteps?"

"Yes, in our case they were only missteps. We had a few. I already told you that we played at being husband and wife."

"Come on!"

"No, don't think the worst. We were—and still are—too young for any kind of perversion. But the last thing on our minds was starting a family. We were two kids living together as man and wife. A year went by, and when no children came, we began to get annoyed, to give each other dirty looks and blame each other silently. I couldn't accept not being a father. I was a man, more than twenty-one years old, and frankly, the idea of being less of a man than other men—less of a man than any brute who has his first child exactly nine months after getting married, if not before—I couldn't accept it."

"But it's no one's fault . . ."

"Obviously, even though I didn't say anything to her, I blamed her and thought, This woman is barren and making a fool of me. I'm sure that she was blaming me, too, and even thinking that . . . who knows?"

"What?"

"Nothing, except that when a year goes by, and another, and another, and there are no children in a marriage, the woman begins to think that it's the husband's fault. She assumes that it wasn't a healthy marriage, that he wasn't physically fit when they got married. It felt like we were enemies, that the devil had invaded our home. Finally, the devil exploded and we began to insult each other. 'You're worthless!' 'You're the one who's worthless!' among other things."

"Is that why, two or three years after you got married, you were in really bad shape, very tense and high-strung, and had to go away to a sanatorium?"

"No, that wasn't the reason, that was something worse."

There was silence. Victor stared at the ground.

"All right, never mind. I don't mean to pry."

"Fine, I'll tell you. Exasperated by those horrible fights with my poor wife, I began to think that the problem had nothing to do with intensity, or whatever you want to call it, but with frequency. Do you understand?"

"I think so."

"I began to eat like a barbarian, devouring everything I thought was especially hearty and nourishing. I ate food heavily seasoned with all kinds of spices—especially if they were supposed to be aphrodisiacal—and to be with my wife as often as possible. And naturally . . ."

"You got sick."

"Of course. And if I hadn't stopped in time and we hadn't come to our senses, I would've disappeared from this world. But I recovered in two ways. I came home from the sanatorium to my wife and we relaxed and resigned ourselves. Little by little, peace and even happiness returned to our home. At the beginning of this new life, after we'd been married for four or five years, we'd occasionally complain about being childless, but eventually we not only comforted each other but got used to it as well. In the end, we didn't miss having children, we even pitied people who did. We got used to each other. You can't possibly understand what I'm saying."

"No, I don't understand."

"I got used to being with my wife, and Elena got used to being with me, like a habit. Everything is regulated in our house. Everything, just like the meals. At twelve o'clock sharp, not a minute before or after, the soup is on the table. We eat almost the same things every day, in the same order and in the same amount. I hate change, so does Elena. In my house, we live by the clock."

"This reminds me of what our friend Luis says about the Romeras. He calls them a bachelor husband and spinster wife."

"He's right, because there's no bachelor more bachelor-like and set in his ways than a married man with no children. Once, to make up for our lack of children, and because our paternal and maternal instincts had never really disappeared, we acquired a dog. You might say we adopted him. But one day, when we saw him die before our eyes with a bone stuck in his throat . . . when we saw those tearful eyes begging us to save his life . . . we were so upset and horrified that we never wanted to get another one, or any other living creature. We contented ourselves with dolls, those big dolls that you've seen in my house, which my Elena dresses and undresses."

"Those won't die on you."

"Exactly. Everything was going well and we were very happy. No crying babies disturbed my sleep. I didn't have to worry about our child being a boy or a girl, or what to do with him or her. Besides, my wife has always been available to me, without the bother of pregnancies or nursing. All in all, a wonderful life."

"It's really not very different, if at all, from—"

"From what? An illicit affair? I think so too. A marriage without children can become a kind of legal affair—very orderly, very sanitary, relatively chaste. After all, that's exactly what it is. Husband and wife, both single, but living together as lovers. That's how the last eleven years, going on twelve, have been. But now . . . do you know what's happened to me?"

"How on earth would I know?"

"You have no idea what's happened?"

"Unless your wife is pregnant . . ."

"That's it exactly! Imagine what a disaster!"

"A disaster? Isn't that what you both wanted so badly?"

"Yes, in the beginning, the first two or three years, not much longer. But now, now . . . the devil is back in our house. We're fighting again. Before, we blamed each other for the sterility of our marriage, now we blame each other for what's happening. And we've started to call it . . . No, I won't tell you."

"Don't tell me if you don't want to."

"We've started to call it 'the Intruder'! I even dreamed it was dying on us one morning with a bone stuck in its throat."

"That's awful."

"You're right, it's awful. Good-bye orderliness, good-bye comfort, good-bye routines. Elena was still throwing up yesterday. It seems to be one of the discomforts associated with the condition people call . . . 'interesting.' Interesting? Vomit is so interesting! Can you imagine anything more gross or disgusting?"

"But isn't she thrilled to become a mother?"

"Elena? As thrilled as I am. This is just a dirty trick that Providence, or Nature, or whatever, is playing on us. It's a joke. If it had come . . . boy or girl, it doesn't matter . . . If it had come when we, innocent lovebirds—more full of vanity than of paternal love—had expected it . . . If it had come when we thought that to be childless was to be inferior to others . . . If it had come then, well, fantastic. But now? Now? I tell you it's a joke. If it weren't for . . ."

"If it weren't for what?"

"I would give it to you to keep Orfeo company."

"Calm down. That's crazy."

"You're right, it's crazy. I'm sorry. But do you think it's fair that after almost twelve years when everything was going so well and we were free of that absurd newlywed pride, that this should happen to us? We were so relaxed, so secure, so confident."

"Come on!"

"You're right, of course, you're right. The worst thing is—you'll never guess—my poor Elena can't help feeling deeply embarrassed. She feels ridiculous."

"I don't see why."

"Neither do I. But that's how she feels. She feels like a fool, and she does things that make me fear for the Intruder . . . or Intrudess."

"Dear God!" Augusto said, alarmed.

"No, no, Augusto, no. We're both still moral people, and Elena, as you know, is deeply religious. She respects God's will, though reluctantly, and is resigned to being a mother. And she'll be a good one, I'm sure about that, a really good mother. But she's so embarrassed that to conceal her condition and hide the pregnancy, I think she's capable of doing things that . . . Anyway, I don't want to think about it. In the meantime, she hasn't been out of the house for a week. She says she's ashamed to go out, she thinks that everyone on the street will stare at her. She wants us to go away, so that if she wants a breath of fresh air and sunshine when she's further along, she won't be around people she knows who might want to come up to her and wish her happiness."

The two friends were quiet.

After the brief silence that marked the end of his story, Victor said, "So, go ahead, Augusto, get married. Maybe something like this will happen to you. Go ahead and marry the piano teacher."

"Who knows?" Augusto said, as though speaking to himself. "Who knows? Maybe if I get married, I'll feel like I have a mother again."

"A mother, yes," Victor said. "For your children, if she has any."

"For me, too. And maybe now you'll find a mother in your wife, Victor, a mother for yourself," Augusto said.

"Forget finding anything. I'm going to lose my nights."

"Or you might get them back, Victor."

"Anyway, I don't know what's happening to me or to us. I think I might eventually resign myself to all of this, but my Elena . . . my poor Elena . . . poor thing."

"See? You're beginning to pity her already."

"Anyway, think long and hard before you get married, Augusto."

They went their separate ways.

Augusto entered the house with his head full of what Don Avito and Victor had said.

He'd almost forgotten about Eugenia, the canceled mortgage, and the girl who did the ironing.

When he entered the house, Orfeo jumped up to greet him. Augusto picked him up, palpated the dog's neck, hugged him closely, and said, "Be careful with bones, Orfeo. Be very careful, all right? I don't want you choking on one. I don't want to watch you die before my very eyes begging for life. You see, Orfeo? Don Avito, the pedagogue, has converted back to his grandparents' religion. It's in his genes. Don Avito can't console himself for the loss of his son and Victor can't console himself for having one. But those eyes of hers, Orfeo, those eyes! How they glared when she said, 'You want to buy me! You want to buy . . . not my love, you can never buy that, but my body! Keep the house!' Buy her body? Her body? My own is too much for me, Orfeo. What I need is a soul. A fiery soul like the one glowing in Eugenia's eyes. Her body . . . her body . . . yes, her body is magnificent, spectacular, divine. But that's because her body is really pure soul, all of it life, meaning, idea. I have too much body, Orfeo, too much because I lack soul. Or maybe I lack soul because I have too much body. I can touch my body, Orfeo, I can feel it and see it. But what about my soul? Where's my soul? Do I have one? I felt it breathe a little only when I held Rosario on my knees. Poor Rosario. When she cried, I cried. Those tears couldn't have come from my body, they came from my soul. The soul is a spring that reveals itself only in tears. Until we truly weep, we don't know whether or not we have a soul. And now, let's sleep, Orfeo, if they let us."

XV

"What have you done, child?" Doña Ermelinda asked her niece.

"What have I done? I'm sure it's what you would've done in my place if you had any shame. To think he wanted to buy me. Buy *me*!"

"Listen, young lady, it's always better to have someone want to buy you than want to sell you. No doubt about that."

"He wanted to buy me. Buy *me*!"

"That wasn't his intention, Eugenia, not at all. He was just being generous, he was being heroic."

"I don't want heroes—I mean men trying to be heroes. When heroism occurs naturally, fine. But when it's calculated? He wanted to buy me. Buy *me*! Me! I'm telling you he'll pay for this. I'll make him pay, that . . ."

"That what? Finish your sentence."

"That insipid fool. As far as I'm concerned, he doesn't exist. He doesn't exist."

"Don't be silly."

"Do you think that guy . . ."

"Who? Uncle Fermín?"

"No, the canary man. Do you think he has anything of substance inside him?"

"At the very least he has some innards in there."

"You think he has innards? Hah! He's hollow. I can tell, he's obviously hollow inside."

"Please, child, let's talk calmly and not say or do anything stupid. Forget about all that. I think you should accept him."

"But I'm not in love with him, *tía*."

"What do you know about love? You have no experience. You may know all there is to know about an eighth or a thirty-second note, but love . . ."

"I think you're just talking to talk, *tía*."

"What do you know about love, child?"

"I'm in love with someone else."

"Someone else? That good-for-nothing Mauricio, whose soul flits around in his body? You call that love? That's 'someone else'? Augusto is your salvation, only Augusto. So refined, so rich, so good."

"That's why I don't love him, because he's as good as you say. I don't like good men."

"Neither do I, child, but . . ."

"But what?"

"We have to marry them. That's why they're born and why they're good—to be our husbands."

"How can I marry him if I don't love him?"

"How? By marrying him! Didn't I marry your uncle?"

"But, *tía* . . ."

"Yes, I think I do now—I seem to—but I'm not sure I loved him when I married him. Look, all this stuff about love comes from books. It was invented to talk and write about. It's poetic nonsense. Marriage is a positive thing. Civil law doesn't even mention love, only marriage. This love business is nothing but music."

"Music?"

"Yes, music. And you know that music barely helps you earn a living. If you don't take advantage of an opportunity like this, you'll be in purgatory for a long time."

"So what? Do I ask you for anything? Aren't I supporting myself? Am I a burden to you?"

"Don't get so worked up. And don't talk like that or we'll have a real fight. Nobody's suggesting anything like that. Everything I say, all my advice, is for your own good."

"Sure, for my own good. Don Augusto has performed that manly act for my own good. A manly act, yes, a manly act! Wanting to buy me. To buy *me*! A manly act. That's what it is, something that men do. I'm beginning to see, *tía*, that men are crass. They're brutes. They lack finesse. They can't even do you a favor without insulting—"

"All men?"

"All men, yes. Real men, of course."

"Ah."

"The others, those who aren't crass or brutish or selfish, aren't men."

"What are they then?"

"I don't know . . . they're queers!"

"You have the strangest theories, child."

"In this house they're contagious!"

"You've never heard your uncle say anything like that."

"No, I came up with it myself after observing men."

"Your uncle, too?"

"My uncle isn't that kind of man."

"Then he's a queer? A queer? Go on, say it."

"No, not that either. My uncle is . . . well, my uncle. I can never get used to the idea that he's really, you know, made of flesh and blood."

"Well, what do you think of your uncle?"

"He's just . . . I don't know how to say it, he's just my uncle. It's as if he didn't really exist."

"You may think that, young lady, but I can tell you, your uncle exists. And how!"

"Brutes, all of them, they're all brutes. Do you know what that boor Martín Rubio said to poor Don Emeterio a few days after he lost his wife?"

"I don't think I heard."

"Well, listen. It was during the epidemic, you know? Everybody was terrified. You wouldn't let me out of the house for days, and I had to drink boiled water. Everyone was avoiding everyone else, and if you saw someone dressed in black, it was as if they had the plague. So, five or six days after losing his wife, poor Don Emeterio had to leave his house. He was dressed in mourning, of course, and he ran into that lout, Martín.

"When Martín saw that Don Emeterio was dressed in black, he stood a safe distance away, as if he was afraid he'd be infected and said, 'What's the matter? Has something happened at home?'

"'Yes,' poor Don Emeterio said, 'I just lost my poor wife.'

"'I'm so sorry. How did she die?'

"'In childbirth,' Don Emeterio said.

"'Oh, thank goodness!' replied the idiot Martín, approaching to shake his hand.

"Quite the gentleman, right? A manly act! I tell you they're all brutes, nothing but brutes!"

"Well, better they should be brutes than lazy bums like that parasite Mauricio, who, for some reason, has brainwashed you. According to my sources—and they're good ones, believe me—I'll be damned if that fool is really in love with you."

"Well, I'm in love with him and that's enough."

"And do you think that good-for . . . I mean your fiancé . . . is really a man? If he were a man, he would have tried hard to find a job and make something of himself a while ago."

"Well, if he isn't a man, I want to make him one. It's true he has that weakness you say, but that may be why I love him. And now, after Don Augusto's manly act—wanting to buy me, to buy *me*!—after that, I've decided to risk everything and marry Mauricio."

"And, what will you live on, you poor child?"

"On my pay. I'll work more than I do now, I'll teach the students I've turned down. Anyway, I've given up the house. I gave it as a present to Don Augusto. It was really nothing more than a whim. It's the house I was born in. Now, without that nightmare of the house and mortgage, I'll put more energy into my lessons. And seeing me teach to support both of us, Mauricio will have to look for a job and start working. I mean, if he has any sense of shame."

"And if he doesn't?"

"If he doesn't, he'll live off me."

"Yes, he'll be the piano teacher's husband."

"So what? He'll be mine, all mine, and the more dependent he is on me, the more he'll be mine."

"Yes, yours, just like a dog. That's what people call 'buying a man.' "

"Hasn't a man wanted to buy me with his money? What's so strange about me, a woman, wanting to buy a man with her wages?"

"All these things you're saying sound a lot like what your uncle calls feminism."

"I don't know about that, and I don't care. But I'm telling you, *tía*, that the man who can buy me hasn't yet been born. Me! Buy *me*!"

At this point in the conversation, the maid entered the room to announce that Don Augusto was waiting to see the señora.

"Him? Go away! I don't want to see him! Tell him I've said all that I have to say."

"Think it over, child, calm down. Don't take it like that. You've misunderstood Don Augusto's intentions."

When Augusto found himself face-to-face with Doña Ermelinda, he began to explain himself. He said he was terribly upset. Eugenia had misunderstood his intentions. He'd paid off the mortgage. The house was free of any financial burdens and she was its lawful owner. If she refused to collect the rent, he wouldn't be able to collect it, so that money would be lost, benefiting no one—or rather it would just be deposited in her name. Besides, he gave up all aspirations to Eugenia's hand in marriage and only wished her happiness. He was even willing to find Mauricio a job so that he wouldn't have to live off his wife's income.

"You have a heart of gold," Doña Ermelinda said.

"All we need now, señora, is for you to convince your niece of my true intent and to forgive me if she thinks it was presumptuous to have paid off the mortgage. There's no point in looking back. If she wants, I'll be best man at her wedding. And then I'll go on a long trip, far away."

Doña Ermelinda called the maid and asked her to tell Eugenia that Don Augusto wanted to speak to her. "The señorita just went out," the maid replied.

XVI

"You're impossible, Mauricio," Eugenia said to her fiancé. They were talking again in the concierge's little room. "You're absolutely impossible. If you continue like this, if you don't shake a leg and start looking for a job so that we can get married, I might do something crazy."

"Like what? Come on, tell me, gorgeous." His hand caressed her neck, winding one of the curls on the nape around his finger.

"Look, if you want, we'll get married just as we are, and I'll keep working . . . for both of us."

"What will people say if I agree to that?"

"I don't care what people say about you!"

"My goodness. That sounds serious!"

"Yes, I don't care about that. I want to put an end to this as soon as possible."

"Is this so bad?"

"Yes, it's bad, it's terrible. If you don't make up your mind, I might . . ."

"Might what? Tell me."

"I might accept Don Augusto's sacrifice."

"Marry him?"

"No, I'd never do that. Take back my house."

"Then do it, baby, do it. If that's the only solution . . ."

"You have the gall to . . ."

"Why not? Poor Don Augusto doesn't seem to be quite right in the head, and since he had this whim, I don't think we should upset him."

"So you . . . ?"

"Of course, baby, of course!"

"A man, after all is said and done!"

"Not as much of a man as you'd like, according to you, but . . . come here."

"Leave me alone, Mauricio. I've told you a hundred times not to . . ."

"Not to be affectionate."

"No, not to be crude. Stop it. If you want more intimacy, stop being so lazy, put some serious effort into finding a job, and you know the rest. Let's see if you can be sensible. Remember, I've already slapped you once."

"It felt great! Come on, gorgeous, slap me again. Here's my face."

"Don't ask me twice."

"Go on, do it!"

"No, I don't want to humor you that way."

"Humor me another way, then."

"I told you not to be crude. And I'm telling you again that unless you hurry up and start looking for a job, I might accept his offer."

"All right, Eugenia. Do you want me to speak to you from the heart and tell you the truth, the whole truth?"

"Tell me."

"I love you very much, I do. I'm crazy about you, but marriage scares me. It scares me to death. I was born lazy, I admit it. Nothing annoys me more than having to work, and I can just tell that if we get married . . . and I assume you want to have kids . . ."

"Of course!"

"Then I'm going to have to work, and work hard because life is expensive. As far as you being the wage earner, that's never, ever going to happen. Mauricio Blanco Clará will never be supported by a woman. But there may be a solution that doesn't require me to work . . . or you, either."

"Go on."

"Well . . . promise not to get mad, sweetheart?"

"Come on, tell me."

"From what I know, and what I've heard you say, this poor Don Augusto is a dolt, a poor devil, you know, a . . ."

"Go on."

"Don't get mad."

"I said, go on."

"Well, as I was saying, he's sort of doomed. Maybe it'd be better not only to accept the house but also . . ."

"Say it. What?"

"Marry him."

"What?" She rose to her feet.

"Marry him, and since he's a pathetic fool, well, problem solved."

"What do you mean, problem solved?"

"Yes, he pays and we . . ."

"We . . . what?"

"Well, we . . ."

"Enough!"

Eugenia left the building, her eyes blazing, thinking, They're brutes, they're brutes! I never would have thought . . . They're brutes! When she got home, she locked herself in her room and burst into tears. Soon she had to lie down, she'd developed a fever.

Mauricio was stunned for a moment, but he recovered quickly, lit a cigarette, walked out onto the street, and whistled at the first pretty girl who passed by. That night he was chatting with a friend about Don Juan Tenorio.

"I don't find the guy very convincing," Mauricio said. "He's just a character in a play."

"That's surprising coming from you, Mauricio. You have a reputation as a Tenorio, a seducer."

"A seducer? Me? People make up some crazy things, Rogelio!"

"What about the piano teacher?"

"Bah! Do you want to know the truth, Rogelio?"

"Tell me."

"All right. Out of a hundred relatively proper relationships—and the one you're talking about is very proper—out of a hundred relationships between a man and a woman, in more than ninety, she's the seducer and he's the seduced."

"What? Are you denying you conquered Eugenia, the pianist?"

"Yes, I'm denying it. I didn't conquer her, she conquered me."

"Seducer!"

"Think what you want. It was her. I found her irresistible."

"It doesn't really matter."

"But I think we're going to break up and that I'm going to be free again. Free of her, of course, because I can't guarantee that another woman won't seduce me. I'm very weak. If I'd been born a woman . . ."

"Why are you breaking up?"

"Because . . . well, because I made a mess of it. I wanted to take things to the next level, you know—without any commitments or consequences—and I think she's going to tell me to get lost. That woman wanted to devour me."

"And she will."

"Who knows? I'm really weak. I was born to be supported by a woman, but with dignity, you know? If not, forget it."

"What do you mean by dignity? Tell me."

"Don't ask me that. Some things are impossible to define."

"That's for sure," Rogelio said emphatically. "What'll you do if the piano teacher breaks up with you?"

"Well, stay single and see if another woman casts her spell on me. I've fallen for a lot of them. But this girl who never gave in, who always maintained a respectable distance, who was decent—she's the most decent girl in the world—she drove me crazy with love. I was completely smitten. She could have done whatever she wanted with me. And now, if she breaks up with me, I'll be deeply hurt, but I'll be free."

"Free?"

"Yes, free. For another."

"I think you're going to get back together."

"Who knows? I doubt it. She has a temper and today I offended her. I really offended her."

XVII

"Augusto, do you remember Don Eloíno Rodríguez de Alburquerque y Álvarez de Castro?" Victor asked.

"The clerk in the Treasury who loved his wine and women, especially on the cheap?"

"That's him. Well, he got married."

"Whoever ended up with him got quite a geezer."

"The amazing thing is how he ended up getting married. Listen to this. I'm sure you know that, despite all the fancy names, Don Eloíno de Alburquerque y Álvarez de Castro barely had enough money to die on—nothing but his salary from the Treasury—and he was in terrible health."

"Because of the life he led."

"So the poor guy has a terminal heart condition, his days are numbered. He's just recovered from a serious setback that has put him at death's door and led him to consider getting married. One more bad turn and he's done for. He was going from one boardinghouse to another, leaving them because, for four *pesetas* a day, you can't expect to eat gourmet delicacies and tasty treats, and he was very demanding . . . and not very clean. After wandering from place to place, he finally landed in one belonging to a respectable older woman. She was older than he was—you know he was closer to sixty than to fifty—and she'd been widowed twice. Her first husband was a carpenter who committed suicide by leaping off a scaffold into the street. She often referred to him as 'her Rogelio.' The second was a sergeant in the carabineers, who left her a little money when he died, which earns her about one *peseta* a day. It was in this widow's house that Don Eloíno began to get sick, very sick—so sick his condition seemed hopeless. He appeared to be dying. First they called in Don José to examine him, and then Don Valentín, but the man was dying. His illness required such constant—and sometimes rather nasty—care, that it was taking up all the landlady's time. Her other boarders were threatening to leave. Don Eloíno couldn't afford to pay more, and the twice-widowed lady was telling him he couldn't stay because it was hurting her business. 'For goodness' sake, señora, have pity,' he apparently told her. 'Where can I go in this condition? Who else is going to take me in? If you throw me out, I'll have to die in a hospital. For God's sake, have a little compassion. I've only got a few days left.' He was convinced he would die soon. But she, of course, told him that her house was not a hospital, that her livelihood depended on her business, and that her business was suffering because of him.

"Just then, another clerk who worked in Don Eloíno's office came up with a great idea. He told Don Eloíno, 'There's only one way to make this good woman let you stay in her house while you're alive.'

"'What's that?'

"'First,' his friend said, 'tell me how sick you are.'

"'Well, I don't think I'll live much longer. My siblings might not get here in time to see me alive.'

"'You think it's that serious?'

"'I feel that I'm dying.'

"'If that's true, there's one way to prevent this kind lady from throwing you out on the street and forcing you to go to a hospital.'

"'What is it?'

"'Marry her.'

"'Marry her? The landlady? Who, me? A Rodríguez de Alburquerque y Álvarez de Castro? Come on, I'm in no mood for jokes.' The idea almost caused him to die on the spot."

"I'm not surprised," Augusto said.

"But as soon as Don Eloíno recovered from the shock, his friend made it clear that if he married the landlady, she would receive a widow's pension of thirteen *duros* a month, which otherwise would be unclaimed and go to the state. So you see . . ."

"Yes, Victor, I know more than one person who's gotten married to prevent the state from keeping his pension. That's civic-mindedness for you."

"But if Don Eloíno angrily rejected this idea, imagine what the landlady had to say. 'I, get married at my age, for the third time, to that old codger? How disgusting!' But, after consulting the doctor, who assured her that Eloíno had only a few days to live, and stating, 'Truthfully, thirteen *duros* a month would come in handy,' she finally agreed. Next, they called the parish priest, kindhearted Don Matías, a saintly man, to convince the dying man to marry her.

"'Yes, I'll talk to him,' Don Matías said. 'The poor man.' And the priest convinced him.

"Then Don Eloíno called his friend Correíta, with whom he'd had a falling-out. He told him he wanted to make peace and asked him to be a witness at the wedding.

"'What? You're getting married, Don Eloíno?'

"'Yes, Correíta. I'm marrying the landlady, Doña Sinfo. I, a Rodríguez de Alburquerque y Álvarez de Castro. Can you believe it? She's agreed to nurse me the last few days of my life. I don't know if my brothers and sisters will get here in time to see me alive. In return she'll receive a widow's pension of thirteen *duros* a month.'

"They say that when Correíta went home, and naturally told his wife, Emilia, the whole story, she said, 'You're an idiot, Pepe. Why didn't you tell him to marry Encarna?' Encarnación is a maid—not very young or pretty—whom Emilia brought to her marriage as a dowry. 'For thirteen *duros*, she would have nursed him as well as that old lady.' Apparently Encarna chimed in, 'You're right, señorita, for thirteen *duros* I would've married him and nursed him during the short time he has left.'

"I think you're making all of this up, Victor."

"I'm not, some things can't be made up, and I haven't told you the best part yet. Don Valentín—the doctor who attended Don Eloíno most often after Don José—told me that one day, when he went to see Don Eloíno, he found the priest, Don Matías, there, in his vestments. He thought the priest had come to administer the last rites, but he was told he was going to perform a marriage. When the doctor returned a little later, the thrice-married landlady bride asked him in a worried, sorrowful voice, 'Please tell me, Don Valentín, will he live? Will he go on living?'

"'No, señora, no. It's a matter of days,' the doctor said.

"'He'll die soon?'

"'Yes, very soon.'

"'Will he really die?'

"That's outrageous!" Augusto said.

"And that's not all," Victor said. "Don Valentín ordered that they give the patient nothing but milk, a little at a time. But Doña Sinfo told a boarder, 'That's ridiculous, I'm going to give him anything he wants. Why deprive him of things he likes when he has so little time left?'

"Then the doctor ordered her to give him enemas, and she said, 'Enemas? How disgusting! To that old geezer? Not me. If he were one of my other two husbands, whom I loved and married because I wanted to . . . But this man? Enemas? Me? Never!' "

"This is unbelievable."

"No, it's true. Some of Don Eloíno's siblings arrived, a brother and sister. The brother was appalled by the disgrace and said, 'To think that my brother, a Rodríguez de Alburquerque y Álvarez de Castro, has married the owner of a boardinghouse on the Calle de Pellejeros. My brother, the son of the former head of the District Court of Zaragoza, of Za-ra-go-za, marrying a . . . Doña Sinfo!' He was horrified.

"The suicide's widow—newly married to the dying man—said, 'Just wait. I can see it now, since we're in-laws, they'll leave without paying for their room and board, even though it's my livelihood.' In the end it seems they did pay her, as did her husband, but they took a cane with a gold handle that had belonged to him."

"Did he die?"

"Yes, a long time afterward. First he got better, lots better."

"The landlady said, 'Don Valentín is to blame for this, he knew how to treat this illness. It would've been better for Don José to have attended him, he didn't understand this illness at all. If he'd treated him, Eloíno would be dead by now and not such a pain.'

"Besides the children from her first marriage, Doña Sinfo also had a daughter from the second marriage to the carabineer. Soon after his marriage to Doña Sinfo, Don Eloíno said to this daughter, 'Come here. Come and let me kiss you. I'm your father now and you're my daughter.'

"'Not your daughter,' her mother said, 'your adopted daughter.'

"'You mean stepdaughter, señora, stepdaughter. Come here. You'll be well-off when I'm gone.'

"I heard that Doña Sinfo grumbled, 'The bastard only said that in order to fondle her. Can you imagine!'

"Then, of course, came the falling-out. 'This was a trick, Don Eloíno, nothing but a trick. I married you only because they assured me you were going to die very soon. If not . . . I've been hoodwinked! They fooled me. I've been fooled!'

"'They fooled me, too, señora. What did you want me to do? Die to please you?'

"'That was the agreement.'

"'I'll die, señora, I'll die sooner than I'd like. I, a Rodríguez de Alburquerque y Álvarez de Castro.'

"Then they fought over a few *cuartos* in the price of the room and board, and she wound up throwing him out of the house.

"'Good-bye, Don Eloíno, I wish you well.'

"'God be with you, Doña Sinfo.'

"At last this lady's third husband died, leaving her 2.15 *pesetas* a day in addition to 500 *pesetas* for mourning. Of course, she didn't spend them on mourning. At most, she had a few masses said for him, out of guilt and gratitude for the thirteen *duros* a month."

"That's quite a story. Dear God."

"Truth is stranger than fiction. You couldn't make up something like that. I'm collecting even more details of this tragicomic funereal farce. At first I considered turning it into a one-act play, but after giving it some thought, I've decided to incorporate it into a novel I'm writing to take my mind off the stress of my wife's pregnancy—the way Cervantes incorporated short tales into *Don Quixote*."

"You're writing a novel?"

"What else should I be doing?"

"What's the plot, if you don't mind my asking?"

"My novel doesn't have a plot, or rather, the plot will reveal itself. It'll create its own plot."

"What do you mean?"

"Look, one day I didn't know what to do with myself, although I desperately needed to do something. I felt a deep yearning—my imagination was restless—and I said, 'I'm going to write a novel, but I'm going to write it the same way we live, unaware of what tomorrow may bring. I sat down, grabbed a few sheets of paper, and wrote down the first thing that occurred to me, without knowing what would happen next—without a plan. My characters will develop through their actions and speech, especially their speech. Their personalities will develop slowly. And sometimes they won't have much of a personality."

"Like me."

"I don't know about that. It'll emerge gradually. I'll go with the flow."

"Is there psychology in it? Descriptions?"

"What there is, is dialogue, mostly dialogue. The important thing is that the characters talk. They should talk a lot, even if they don't say much."

"That must've been Elena's idea."

"Why?"

"Because once, when she asked me to recommend a novel to read for fun, I remember she wanted one with lots of snappy dialogue."

"Sure. Whenever she reads a book with long descriptions, sermons or narrative passages, she skips over those parts, saying, 'Padding, padding, nothing but padding!' For her, the only thing that isn't padding is the dialogue. Of course, you can deliver a sermon through dialogue."

"Why does she prefer dialogue so much?"

"People like conversation for its own sake, even if it's inane. Some people can't sit through a thirty-minute speech, but they'll spend three hours chatting in a café. Conversation has its charms, talking just to talk, even with interruptions or incomplete thoughts."

"I find the tone of speeches wearisome too."

"We enjoy conversation, especially conversation that sounds natural, when it doesn't seem like the author's speaking, annoying us with his personality and diabolical ego, even though I, of course, am speaking through my characters."

"Well, up to a certain point."

"What do you mean?"

"At the beginning, you'll think you're leading them by the hand, but, by the end, you might acknowledge that they're leading you. Characters often end up toying with an author."

"Maybe, but I plan to put whatever occurs to me in this novel, whatever it might be."

"Then it won't be a novel."

"No. It'll be . . . it'll be a . . . *nivola*."

"What's a nivola?"

"I once heard the poet Manuel Machado, Antonio's brother, tell how he took one of his sonnets to Eduardo Benot, to read to him. The sonnet was written in alexandrines or some other unusual verse.

"He read it to him and Eduardo said, 'That's not a sonnet.'

"'No, señor,' Machado replied, 'it's not a sonnet, it's a *sunnit*.'

"In the same way, my novel isn't going to be a novel, but rather a . . . what did I call it? *Navilo? Nebulo?* No, a nivola, That's it, a nivola. No one will be able to say that I'm violating the rules of the genre. I'm inventing a new genre—I only need to give it a different name—and it will be subject to whatever rules I like. And include lots of dialogue."

"What about when a character is alone?"

"Then . . . a monologue. And, to make it seem like a dialogue, I'll invent a dog for the person to talk to."

"You know what, Victor? I feel like you're inventing *me*."

"I might be."

After Victor and Augusto parted, Augusto thought, Is my life a novel or a nivola or what? All that's happening to me—and to the people around me—is it reality or fiction? Maybe this is all God's dream, or whoever's, and it will disappear the moment He wakes up. Maybe that's why we pray and sing hymns to Him, to lull and rock Him to sleep. Maybe the liturgy of all the world's religions is only a way to soothe God as He dreams, so that He doesn't wake up and stop dreaming us. Oh, my Eugenia! And my Rosarito!

"Hello, Orfeo."

Orfeo had come out to greet him. He was jumping up and down, trying to crawl up his legs. Augusto picked him up and the puppy began to lick his hand.

"Señor," said Liduvina. "Rosarito is here with the laundry, waiting for you."

"Why didn't you take care of the bill yourself?"

"I don't know. I told her you wouldn't be long and that if she wanted to wait . . ."

"But you always take care of it."

"Yes, but . . . you know."

"Liduvina! Liduvina!"

"You should pay her yourself."

"I'll be right there."

XVIII

"Hello, Rosarito!" Augusto said as soon as he saw her.

"Good afternoon, Don Augusto." The girl's voice was calm and clear and so were her eyes.

"Why didn't you take care of the bill with Liduvina as you always do when I'm not home?"

"I don't know. She told me to wait. I thought you wanted to talk to me."

Could this girl be that naive or what? Augusto wondered, unsure how to respond.

It was an awkward moment, filled with uneasy silence.

"What I want, Rosario, is for you to forget about the other day. Don't give it another thought, understand?"

"All right, whatever you say."

"That was insane, truly insane. I didn't know what I was saying or doing. I still don't."

He stepped toward the girl.

She waited placidly, apparently resigned. Augusto sat down on the sofa and said, "Come here." He told her to sit on his lap like before and stared into her eyes for a long time. She looked back at him calmly, but her body was trembling like an aspen leaf.

"Are you shaking?"

"Me? No, I think it's you who—"

"Stop shaking. Relax."

"Don't make me cry again."

"I think you want me to make you cry again. Tell me, do you have a boyfriend?"

"What kind of a question is . . . ?"

"Tell me, do you?"

"Not a real boyfriend, no."

"No boy your age has shown any interest in you?"

"You know how it is, Don Augusto."

"What did you say to him?"

"Some things are private."

"True enough. Tell me, do you love each other?"

"For God's sake, Don Augusto!"

"Look, if you're going to cry, I'll leave you alone."

The girl leaned her head forward onto Augusto's chest, hiding her face, and burst into tears, trying to muffle her sobs. This girl is going to pass out on me, he thought, stroking her hair.

"Calm down, calm down."

"What about that woman?" Rosarito asked, without lifting her head, choking back her sobs.

"Oh, you remember? Well, that woman rejected me completely. I never did win her heart, and now I've lost her completely."

The girl raised her head and looked closely at his face to see if he was telling the truth.

"You want to fool me," she whispered.

"I want to fool you? Oh, I see. So that's what you think? Didn't you say you had a boyfriend?"

"I didn't say anything."

"Relax, relax." He placed her next to him on the sofa, stood up, and began to pace around the room. But when he looked back, he saw that the poor girl was pale and trembling. He understood that she felt vulnerable sitting there alone on the sofa a few feet in front of him—like a criminal before a judge—that she felt faint.

"It's true," he said. "The closer we are to each other, the safer we feel."

He sat down, pulled her onto his lap, put his arms around her, and hugged her tightly. The poor girl put one arm over his shoulder, as if to lean on him, and hid her face against Augusto's chest again. His heart was beating so hard it scared her.

"Are you ill, Don Augusto?"

"Is anyone really well?"

"Should I ask them to bring you something?"

"No, it's fine. I know what's wrong with me. I need to travel." And, after a brief silence, "Will you come with me?"

"Don Augusto!"

"Don't call me 'Don.' Will you come with me?"

"If you want me to."

A fog invaded Augusto's mind, blood began to throb in his temples. He felt a heavy weight on his chest. To shake it off, he began to kiss Rosario's eyes, which she had to close.

Suddenly he stood up and said as he walked away, "Leave me. Go. I'm afraid."

"What are you afraid of?"

The girl's sudden composure scared him even more.

"I'm afraid—I'm not sure of whom—of you, of me, of whatever! Of Liduvina. Look, go now, go. But you'll come back, won't you? You'll come back?"

"Whenever you want."

"And you'll go on a trip with me?"

"If you want me to."

"Then go. Go now."

"And that woman . . . ?"

Augusto rushed toward the girl, who was now standing, grabbed her, held her against his chest, pressed his dry lips against hers without really kissing her, and stood there for a moment, his mouth clamped onto hers, shaking his head from side to side.

Then he let go of her and said, "Go now. Go."

Rosario left. As soon as she'd gone, Augusto, as exhausted as if he'd run for miles in the mountains, threw himself on his bed, turned off the light, and began his monologue.

I've been lying to her and to myself, he thought. It's always the same. It's all a fantasy and nothing but a fantasy. As soon as we talk, we lie, and as soon as we talk to ourselves . . . I mean, as soon as we think, knowing that we're thinking, we lie to ourselves. The only real truth is physiological. Words, these social constructs, were made for lying. In fact, I've heard one philosopher say that truth, like language, is also a social construct. Truth is what everybody believes, and in believing the same thing, we understand one another. Any social construct is a lie.

He felt something licking his hand and said, "Oh, you're here already, Orfeo? Since you don't talk, you don't lie. I'm pretty sure you don't misconstrue things, so you don't even lie to yourself. Although, being a domestic animal, you've probably acquired some human traits. We do nothing but lie and make ourselves feel important. Words and all other conventional forms of expression, like hugging and kissing, were created to magnify all our feelings and perceptions, perhaps so we can believe them. We're all just playing our parts. We're all characters, we're masks, we're actors. None of us enjoy, or even endure, what we say or claim we enjoy and endure. Otherwise, we wouldn't be able to live. Down deep we're all very calm, just like I am now, performing my part alone in my play, both as an actor and spectator. The only deadly pain is physical pain. Our only real truth is physiological. No words or lies there."

He heard a soft knock at the door.

"What is it?"

"Aren't you eating dinner tonight?" Liduvina asked.

"Of course. I'll be right there."

"And later I'll fall asleep, like every other night, and so will she. Will Rosarito sleep? Did I upset her calm spirit? That unaffected quality she has . . . is it genuine innocence or cunning? Maybe there's nothing more cunning than innocence or more innocent than cunning. Yes, I've always assumed that really, there's nothing more . . . how should I put it? . . . more cynical than innocence. That calm when she gave in to me, *that* scared me. I'm not sure what I was afraid of. That was pure innocence. And when she said, 'And that woman?' Jealousy, right? Jealousy? There probably can't be love without jealousy. Jealousy reveals our love to us. Even if a woman is deeply in love with a man, or a man with a woman, they don't realize it, they don't tell themselves that they are—they don't really fall in love—until he sees her look at another man or she sees him look at another woman. If there were only one man and one woman in the world, no one else, they would never fall in love with each other. Besides, there always has to be a go-between, a Celestina, and society plays that role. *El gran Galeoto*! That's it! Yes, *The Great Mediator*! That's perfect. If only because of its language. That's why this whole business of love is just one more lie. And the physical side of it? Hah! That's not love either or anything like it. That's why it's not a lie, it's real. But . . . come on, Orfeo, let's have dinner. There's no doubt that's real."

XIX

Two days later Augusto was informed that a lady wished to speak to him. He went out to greet her and discovered it was Doña Ermelinda.

"I'm surprised to see you here," he said.

"Well, since you haven't come by to see us again . . ."

"Please understand, señora," Augusto said, "that I couldn't go back after what happened the last two times, when I spoke to Eugenia alone, and when she refused to see me. I'll honor what I've said and done, but I can't go back there."

"Eugenia asked me to see you."

"She did?"

"Yes. I don't know what's happened with that boyfriend of hers, but she doesn't want to hear anything about him. She's furious with him, and the other day when she came home, she locked herself in her room and refused to eat any dinner. Her eyes were red from crying, from shedding those hot tears, you know, the furious ones."

"Are there different kinds of tears?"

"Of course. There are tears that soothe and refresh and tears that torment and burn. She'd been crying and refused any dinner. And she kept repeating the line about all men being brutes, nothing but brutes. She's been down in the dumps for days, in a horrible mood. Then yesterday she asked to speak to me and told me that she regretted what she'd said to you, that she'd gone too far and been unfair to you. She now sees that your intentions were honorable and noble. She's not asking you to forgive her for saying that you wanted to buy her, but to know that she doesn't believe that anymore. She asked me to stress that. She wants you to know that she said it only because she was upset and feeling spiteful. But she doesn't believe it."

"I believe that she doesn't believe it."

"Then she asked me to find out, diplomatically . . ."

"It's best not to be diplomatic, especially with me."

"She begged me to find out whether you'd mind if she accepted her house as a gift, no strings attached."

"What do you mean, no strings attached?"

"If she accepted it simply as a gift."

"If I give it to her as a gift, how else should she accept it?"

"She says she's willing to accept it. To show her goodwill and how sorry she is for what she said. She's willing to accept your generous gift, as long as it doesn't imply . . ."

"Enough, señora, please. It seems that unwittingly you're both about to offend me again."

"I don't mean to offend you."

"They say that sometimes the worst insults are unintentional."

"I don't understand."

"It's crystal clear. I once went to a party where an acquaintance of mine didn't even greet me. When I left, I complained to a friend and he said, 'Don't be so surprised, he didn't do it on purpose. He didn't even notice you were there.'

"'That's even more insulting,' I said. 'Not noticing me is worse than not greeting me.'

"'It wasn't intentional,' he said. 'His head's always in the clouds.'

"I replied, 'The worst insults are the so-called unintentional ones, and there's nothing ruder than to disappear into your own world when you're surrounded by others.' It's like what people stupidly call 'unintentional forgetfulness,' señora, as if it were possible to forget something intentionally. Unintentional forgetfulness is usually just rudeness."

"What's your point?"

"My point, Doña Ermelinda, is that after apologizing for insulting me by saying that I was trying to buy her with my gift and extort her gratitude, I don't understand what she means by accepting it 'with no strings attached.' What strings is she referring to?"

"Don't get upset, Don Augusto."

"Why shouldn't I get upset, señora? Why not? Is this girl just going to make fun of me and toy with me?" As he said this, Rosarito flashed through his mind.

"For God's sake, Don Augusto!"

"I've already said that the mortgage is taken care of. I've paid it off. If she doesn't manage the house, no one will. I've washed my hands of it. I couldn't care less if she thanks me or not."

"Please, Don Augusto, calm down. She wants to make peace with you and be friends."

"Sure, now that she's at war with the other guy, right? I was the other guy before. Now I'm the one, aren't I? She wants to lure me in again."

"I never said anything like that."

"No, but I can guess."

"Well, you're completely wrong. Right after my niece told me everything I've told you, when I tried to suggest that since she's broken up with that lazy oaf, she might consider . . . you know."

"Winning me back?"

"Exactly. When I suggested that, she told me a thousand times, 'No, no, no.' She values and respects you as a friend but doesn't want to marry you. She has to be in love with the man she marries."

"And she could never fall in love with me, could she?"

"She didn't say that in so many words."

"Please. You're being diplomatic again."

"What do you mean?"

"You've come not only to get me to forgive the girl but also to see if I'm still interested in marrying her, right? You've worked it all out, haven't you? And she'll resign herself . . ."

"I swear to you, Don Augusto, I swear on my mother's sacred memory, may she rest in peace, I swear . . ."

"The second commandment forbids swearing."

"I swear to you that you're forgetting—unintentionally, of course—who I am. Who Ermelinda Ruiz y Ruiz is."

"If that's true . . ."

"Yes, it is, yes." She said this so sincerely that he had to believe her.

"Well then, tell your niece that I accept her explanations and am deeply grateful for them. I'll continue to be her friend, a loyal and trustworthy one, but nothing more than that. Just a friend. Don't tell her that I'm not a piano she can play whenever she feels like it, I'm not a man she can pick up today and drop tomorrow, I'm not a replacement or a second fiddle, or leftovers . . ."

"Don't get so worked up."

"I'm not getting worked up. All right, we can still be friends."

"And you'll come visit us soon?"

"As far as visiting you . . ."

"If you don't, the poor thing won't believe me. She'll be hurt."

"It's just that I'm thinking of going on a long trip, very far away."

"Then come say good-bye before you leave."

"We'll see."

They parted and when Doña Ermelinda returned home, she told her niece about the conversation she'd had with Augusto. There's someone else, Eugenia thought, I'm sure of it. Now I have to win him back.

Once Augusto found himself alone, he began to pace around the room. She wants to play me like a piano, he thought. She drops me, she picks me up, she drops me again. I was the backup. No matter what she says, she wants to rope me in again, maybe for revenge, maybe to make the other guy jealous so he'll fall head over heels in love with her again. As if I were a puppet, a thing, a nobody. I'm my own person, absolutely. I'm me! Yes, I'm me! Sure, I've got her, Eugenia, to thank for waking up my ability to love. But now that she roused and stirred it up, I don't need her anymore. There are plenty of women.

At this point he couldn't help smiling. He remembered what Victor said when Gervasio, newly married, announced that he was going to spend some time in Paris with his wife. "He's taking his wife to Paris? That's like taking beer to Germany!" which Augusto found hilarious.

There are plenty of women, he repeated to himself. And isn't Rosarito—this modern version of eternal Eve—isn't her cunning innocence, her innocent cunning, adorable? She's such a charming girl. Eugenia brought me down from the abstract to the concrete, but Rosario led me to the generic, and there are so many attractive women. So many . . . so many Eugenias, so many Rosarios! No, no one toys with me, especially a woman. I'm me! My soul may be small but it's mine. He felt that this acknowledgment of self-worth caused his ego to swell bigger and bigger and the house to feel cramped, so he left the house to seek some relief and breathing space.

He stepped onto the street with the sky overhead and saw people coming and going for business and pleasure, ignoring him. This was unintentional, of course. They probably paid no attention to him because they were strangers. As soon as his foot touched the pavement, he felt himself, the self that had declared, "I'm me!" start to shrink and become smaller and smaller. It was not only folding up in his body but also searching for a tiny corner in which to curl up and disappear.

The street was like a movie theater and he felt like part of a movie, like a shadow, a ghost. Whenever he plunged into a crowd and lost himself among masses of people coming and going—who didn't know or pay any attention to him—he felt as though he were bathing outdoors, surrounded by nature under the open sky, with winds blowing in all directions.

He felt like himself only when he was alone. That's when he could tell himself—maybe even convince himself—"I'm me." When he was with other people in the middle of a busy, preoccupied crowd, he didn't feel like himself, he lost touch with himself.

In this frame of mind he arrived at the modest garden of the plaza tucked away in the secluded neighborhood where he lived. The plaza was a peaceful haven where there were always children playing. No streetcars passed through it and very few cars. Elderly people sat in the sun on mild autumn afternoons, when the north wind blew the leaves of the dozen chestnut trees confined there, causing them to dart along the flagstones or cover the wooden benches painted green, the color of fresh foliage. Those domesticated urban trees, standing at attention in straight lines, watered by an irrigation ditch when it didn't rain, extending their roots under the plaza's flagstones . . . Those imprisoned trees waiting to see the sun rise and set over rooftops . . . Those caged trees that perhaps yearned for a distant forest . . . Augusto felt mysteriously drawn to them. Birds sang in their branches, city birds that learn to flee from children and sometimes approach the old folks who offer them bread crumbs.

How many times, sitting there alone and lonely on one of the plaza's green benches, had he watched the setting sun blaze over a rooftop, occasionally glimpsing the outline of a black cat on top of a chimney against the incandescent gold of the sun's magnificent sunset? Meanwhile, in the fall, yellow leaves wide as grape leaves, laminated and stiff like mummified hands, rained down on the small gardens in the center of the plaza with their flowerpots and borders.

The children played among the dry leaves, sometimes collecting them, unaware of the flaming sunset.

That day, when he arrived at the tranquil plaza, Augusto brushed the dry leaves off a bench—it was autumn—and sat down. He looked over and saw children playing nearby as usual. One of them placed another close to the trunk of a chestnut tree and said, "You were a prisoner here, locked up by robbers."

"But I—" the other boy complained.

The first one said, "Not the real you."

Augusto didn't want to hear any more. He got up and moved to another bench. We adults play the same game, he thought. "You're not you." "I'm not me." Are these poor trees themselves? They shed their leaves much earlier than their brothers in the mountains, and they turn into skeletons. Electric lights shine their bright beams on them, projecting their spindly shadows onto the pavement. Trees lit by electricity? In the spring, the lights make the treetops look strange and otherworldly, as if they were metallic. Here, there are no breezes. These poor trees can't even enjoy one of those black country nights, those moonless nights, tucked under a blanket of flickering stars. It's as if man said to each of these trees as he planted it, "You're not you." And as a constant reminder, he turned on the lights at night, so they wouldn't be able to sleep. Poor sleepless trees. No, no one is going to toy with me that way.

He got off the bench and began to walk up and down the streets as though he were sleepwalking.

XX

Should he go on a trip, yes or no? He'd already said he was going, first impulsively to Rosarito, just to say something—or rather as an excuse to ask if she would go with him—and then to Doña Ermelinda, to prove to her . . . what? What was he trying to prove by telling her he was going on a trip? It didn't matter. He'd let down his guard twice. He'd said he was going on a long trip, far away, and he was a man of character. He was who he was. Did he have to keep his word?

Men who keep their word speak first and think later. They follow through whether or not it seems like a good idea once they've had time to think it over. Men who keep their word never change their minds or take back what they've said, and he'd said he was going on a long trip, far away. A long, faraway trip? Why? What for? How? Where? Just then Liduvina announced that a young lady was waiting to see him.

"A young lady?"

"Yes," Liduvina said. "I think it's . . . the piano teacher."

"Eugenia?"

"Yes, her."

He was caught off guard. The idea of sending her away flashed through his mind. They could say he wasn't home. She's come to conquer me again, to play with me like a puppet, he thought. She wants to lure me in and replace the other guy. No, I'd better show her I'm strong, he decided.

"Tell her I'll be right there."

He was amazed at her audacity. You have to admit she's quite a woman, he thought. She really is something. What nerve, what tenacity, what eyes! But no, I won't give in. She won't seduce me again.

When Augusto entered the room, Eugenia was standing. He motioned for her to sit down, but before she did, she said, "You've been deceived as much as I have, Don Augusto." The poor man was taken aback, he didn't know what to say. They both sat down and there was a brief silence.

"That's right, Don Augusto. You've been deceived about me and I've been deceived about you. That's the truth."

"But we've talked to each other, Eugenia."

"Forget what I said to you. What's done is done."

"What's done is always done. It can't be undone."

"You know what I mean, and I don't want you to read anything into my acceptance of your generous gift."

"And I don't want *you* to misinterpret my motives for giving you the gift."

"So we agree to trust each other. And now, since we should speak frankly, I have to tell you that after everything that's happened and all that I've said, there's no way I can repay your generous gift with anything but gratitude. Just as you, for your part, I think . . ."

"You're right, señorita. For my part, after all that's happened and what you said the last time we met, after what your aunt told me and what I can guess, I couldn't put a price on my generosity even if I wanted to."

"So we agree?"

"Completely, señorita."

"And we can be friends again? Good friends? Real friends?"

"Absolutely."

Eugenia extended her delicate hand, as white and cold as snow, with tapered fingers made to rule keyboards, and he grasped it in his, which was trembling.

"So we'll be friends, Don Augusto, good friends, although this friendship for me . . ."

"What?"

"Well, others might think . . ."

"What? Speak up, tell me."

"Anyway, after recent painful experiences, I've given up on certain things."

"Speak clearly, señorita. There's no point in beating around the bush."

"All right, Don Augusto. I'll speak very clearly. Do you think anyone will want to have a romantic relationship with me now that most of our acquaintances know you've paid off my mortgage and given me the house as a gift?"

This woman is diabolical, Augusto thought. He looked down and stared at the floor, speechless. When he looked up a moment later, he saw Eugenia wipe away a furtive tear.

"Eugenia!" he exclaimed, his voice quivering.

"Augusto," she whispered back.

"What do you want us to do?"

"Nothing, it's fate, that's all. It toys with us. This is a disaster."

Augusto got up from his chair and sat down on the sofa next to Eugenia.

"Look, Eugenia, for God's sake, don't play with me like this. You're the fate, there's no fate here but you. You have me coming and going and spinning like a top. It's you, you drive me crazy. You make me break my strongest promises to myself. I'm not myself around you."

He put his arm around her neck, drew her close, and held her tightly against his chest.

She calmly took off her hat.

"Yes, Augusto, fate has brought us to this point. Neither of us can be unfaithful or untrue to who we are. You can't appear to be buying me, as I told you when I was upset, and I can't appear to be using you as a replacement, a runner-up, a second fiddle, as you told my aunt. I only want to reward your generosity . . ."

"Why should we care about appearances, my sweet Eugenia? Who's going to judge us?"

"We are."

"So what, my darling?"

He pulled her close again and began to kiss her eyes and forehead. Their breathing grew louder.

"Let go! Let go of me!" she said, regaining her composure and smoothing her hair.

"No, you . . . you . . . Eugenia . . . you . . ."

"No, I can't."

"Don't you love me?"

"Love? Who knows what love is?" she said. "I don't. I'm not sure what it is."

"What's this, then?" he asked.

"This is just a moment of weakness caused by remorse. Who knows? Some things need to be tested. Besides, Augusto, didn't we say that we would be friends, good friends, nothing more?"

"Yes, but . . . what about all you're giving up? The fact that because you accepted my gift and because you're a friend of mine—nothing but a friend—no one will want to marry you?"

"That doesn't matter anymore. I've made up my mind."

"Maybe after breaking up with—"

"Maybe . . ."

"Eugenia! Eugenia!"

Just then they heard a knock at the door. Augusto, shaken, his face flushed, said curtly, "What is it?"

"Rosario is waiting to see you," Liduvina's voice replied.

The color drained from his face. He was livid.

"Ah," Eugenia said. "I'm in the way. Rosario is waiting for you. You see how we can only be friends, very good friends?"

"But, Eugenia—"

"Rosario is waiting for you."

"When you rejected me, Eugenia—and you *did* reject me, accusing me of wanting to buy you and telling me you were in love with someone else—what did you expect me to do when, after seeing you, you taught me to love? Haven't you ever heard of spite or what happens to love when it is snubbed or spurned?"

"Come, Augusto, give me your hand. We'll see each other again, but let's let bygones be bygones."

"No, let's not let bygones be bygones. No!"

"All right, fine. Rosario is waiting for you."

"For God's sake, Eugenia . . ."

"No, there's really nothing unusual about this. Somebody used to wait for me, too . . . Mauricio. We'll see each other again. Let's take things seriously and be true to ourselves."

She put on her hat and offered her hand to Augusto, who raised it to his lips and covered it with kisses. He walked her to the door and watched her go down the stairs, elegantly and confidently. When she reached the landing she looked up at him one last time before leaving. He turned and went back into his study. When he saw Rosario standing there with the laundry basket, he said brusquely, "What is it?"

"I think, Don Augusto, that that woman is deceiving you."

"What do you care?"

"I care about everything that concerns you."

"You mean that you think I'm deceiving *you*."

"I don't care about that."

"You want me to believe you're not jealous, after I've gotten your hopes up?"

"If you knew how I was raised, Don Augusto, and what my family was like, you'd understand that even though I'm young, I never get jealous. Girls in my position . . ."

"Hush!"

"Fine, but I'm telling you, that woman is deceiving you. If it weren't true, and if you loved her and wanted to marry her, I'd be happy for you."

"Really?"

"Really."

"How old are you?"

"Nineteen."

"Come here." He put his hands on her shoulders and placed her directly in front of him.

They stood face-to-face and he stared into her eyes. But it was Augusto whose face grew pale, not hers.

"The truth is, sweetheart, that I don't understand you."

"I believe you."

"I don't know whether this is innocence, malice, ridicule, preco-cious spitefulness . . ."

"This is nothing but tenderness."

"Tenderness? Why?"

"You want to know why? You won't be offended if I tell you? You promise not to be offended?"

"Go ahead, tell me."

"Well, because . . . because you're a poor unhappy man."

"You too?"

"Don't believe me if you don't want to, but you should trust this girl. Trust Rosario. No one is more loyal to you, not even Orfeo."

"You'll always be loyal?"

"Always."

"No matter what?"

"Yes, no matter what."

"You, you're the real . . ." he said and tried to embrace her.

"No, not now. When you calm down. And when you haven't just . . ."

"Right. I understand."

They said good-bye and Augusto found himself alone again. Between this one and that one, I'm going to lose my mind, he thought. I'm not myself anymore.

When Liduvina served him dinner, she said, "I think you should go into politics. It would get your mind off things."

"What on earth made you think of that?"

"You'd be better off distracting yourself than having someone distract you. That's for sure."

"Well, then, call your husband. Call Domingo as soon as I'm done with dinner and tell him I want to play a game of *tute* to get my mind off things."

As they were playing, Augusto suddenly put his cards on the table and said, "So, tell me, Domingo. If a man is in love with two or more women at the same time, what should he do?"

"It depends."

"What do you mean, it depends?"

"Well, if he has lots of money and lots of nerve, he should marry all of them. If not, he shouldn't get married at all."

"He can't marry all of them."

"Anything is possible if you have lots of money."

"What if they find out?"

"They won't care."

"You don't think a woman minds sharing her husband's love with another woman?"

"She'll be happy with the love he gives her, señor, as long as he doesn't limit the money she spends. Women hate to be told how much they can spend on food and clothes and luxuries. But if he lets her spend as much as she wants . . . On the other hand, if she bears his children . . ."

"If she bears his children, then what?"

"That's what arouses real jealousy, señor—children. Mothers can't tolerate other mothers, even other potential mothers. They can't stand to have their kids slighted for other kids or for another woman. But if they don't have kids and the man doesn't limit the amount she can spend on food or clothes, or glamour and extravagances . . . hah! . . . she'll even feel relieved. If a man has a woman who costs him a lot, and another who doesn't cost him anything, the more expensive one isn't going to be jealous of the cheaper one. And if on top of not costing anything, the cheaper one also brings in some money . . . If he gives one woman the money he gets from the other one, then . . ."

"Then, what?"

"Then everyone will get along fine. Believe me, there are no female Othellos."

"Or male Desdemonas."

"Maybe not."

"You say the most amazing things."

"Before I married Liduvina and came to work for you, I served in the homes of many wealthy people. I cut my teeth in them."

"Is love the same for people in your social class?"

"In my class we don't allow ourselves certain luxuries."

"What do you call luxuries?"

"Things you see on the stage or read about in novels."

"Crimes of passion motivated by jealousy are so rarely seen in your social class."

"That's because those fools go to the theater and read novels. If they didn't . . ."

"What?"

"We all like to play different roles. No one is who they are, only the person others think he is."

"You're quite the philosopher."

"That's what my old boss used to say. But I agree with Liduvina. You should go into politics."

XXI

"You're right," Don Antonio said to Augusto that afternoon when they were talking in a quiet corner of the club. "You're right. I have a very painful secret in my life. You've sensed it. You've been to my poor home—if you can call it a home—only a few times, but you must have noticed . . ."

"Yes, something strange. A vague sense of sadness that attracted me to it."

"Despite my children, my poor children, it must have seemed like a childless home to you, maybe even one without a husband and wife."

"I don't know."

"We moved here from far away, hoping to escape certain things. But some things stay with you. They surround and envelop you like a mysterious energy. My poor wife . . ."

"Yes, in your wife's face I see a lifetime of . . ."

"Of suffering. Go ahead, say it. Anyway, my friend, you've shown us more kindness and compassion than anyone else. I'm not sure why, maybe because you sympathize with us. I keep thinking it would be a relief to confide in someone, so I'm going to tell you all my trials and tribulations. That woman, the mother of my children, isn't my wife."

"I suspected as much. But really, if she's the mother of your children, if you live as man and wife, then she's your wife."

"No, I have another wife, a so-called legitimate wife. I'm married, but not to the woman you know. And this woman, the mother of my children, is also married, but not to me."

"Ah! A double—"

"No, a quadruple. You'll see. I was in love, madly in love, with the woman I married. She was a quiet, reserved little thing. She didn't talk much. It always seemed like she wanted to say more than she did. She had the sweetest sleepy blue eyes. They woke up only occasionally, but when they did, sparks flew out of them. Every part of her was like that: her heart, her soul, her entire body. They seemed to be dormant. They would wake up suddenly, as if startled, but soon fall asleep again once the burst of vitality had passed—and her vitality was incredible. Afterward it was as if nothing had happened, as if she'd forgotten everything.

"It was as if we were always starting our life over from the beginning, as if I were forever courting her. She'd accepted my proposal in an altered state, like an epileptic fit, and I think she married me in front of the altar in the midst of another one. I could never get her to say whether she loved me or not. I would ask her often, both before and after we were married, and she'd always say, 'What kind of a question is that? Don't be silly.' Other times she said that the verb 'to love' was used only in plays or in books, and that if I'd written 'I love you' to her, she would have told me to get lost. Our first two years of marriage were strange. Every day I tried to win over that sphinxlike woman again. We had no children. Then one night she didn't come home. I went crazy and looked for her everywhere, and the next day I received a short, brusque letter telling me she'd fled far away with another man."

"You didn't see it coming? You had no inkling?"

"None. My wife often went out by herself, to her mother's or to see friends, and her odd lack of emotion kept me from being suspicious. I never knew what was going on inside that sphinx's head. The man she ran away with was married. He abandoned his wife and young daughter to run off with mine, and he stole his wife's large fortune, which he'd used to satisfy his every whim. So he not only abandoned his wife but he also ruined her financially. In that curt, short, heartless letter I received from my wife, she mentioned the state in which her abductor had left this poor other woman. Abductor or abductee? Who knows? For a few days I couldn't sleep, I couldn't eat or rest. I walked around remote neighborhoods in the city and was on the verge of giving in to the most shameful, degenerate vices. But when my grief began to fade and I could think clearly again, I remembered that other poor victim, the woman who'd been left helpless, robbed of both love and money. Since my wife was responsible for her bad luck, I felt I should offer her some financial help, especially since God has made me wealthy."

"I can guess what happened next, Don Antonio."

"Anyway, I went to see her. Imagine what our first meeting was like. We cried over our misfortunes, which were really one and the same. I thought, That man left this woman for my wife, and I felt—why not tell you the truth?—a deep satisfaction, something inexplicable, as if I'd understood how to pick a better wife than he did, and he knew it. And she, his wife, later told me she was thinking the same thing, only in reverse. I offered to help her financially any way I could. At first she turned me down. 'I'll get a job to support myself and my daughter,' she said. But I insisted so much that she finally gave in. I suggested that we move far away from our hometowns and that she come live with me as my housekeeper. After taking some time to think it over, she agreed."

"Then, naturally, after living in the same house . . ."

"No, that came later, sometime later, probably as a result of living together combined with vindictiveness and spite, whatever. At the time I became attached, not so much to her as to her daughter, my wife's lover's unfortunate daughter. I loved her like a father, with a fierce paternal love I feel even now. I love her as much—maybe even more—than my own children. I'd pick her up and hug her tightly, showering her with kisses, and I'd cry and cry over her. And the poor little girl would say, 'Why are you crying, daddy?' I'd asked her to call me daddy and to think of me as her father. When she saw me cry like that, her poor mother would cry too. Sometimes our tears would mingle over the little blond head of my wife's lover's child, the daughter of the man who stole my happiness.

"One day," Don Antonio continued, "I found out that my wife had had a son with her lover. I was consumed with rage. I suffered like I've never suffered before. I thought I would lose my mind and commit suicide. Until then I'd never felt how brutal jealousy could be. The wound in my soul, which I thought had healed, opened and bled. It bled fire. I'd lived with my wife, my legitimate wife, for two years, and nothing. And now, that thief . . . I imagined that my wife had finally awakened and was burning with lust. The other woman, the one I lived with, sensed something and asked, 'What's wrong?' 'Leave me alone,' I said. But I ended up telling her everything and she started shaking as I spoke. I think I infected her with my rabid jealousy."

"So, of course, after that . . ."

"No, that came later, in a different way. One day, we were both with the little girl. She was on my lap and I was telling her stories, kissing her and saying silly things. Her mother came up to us and began caressing her too. Then the poor little thing put one hand on my shoulder and the other on her mother's and said, 'Daddy, Mommy, why don't you bring me a little brother to play with, like the other girls have, so I won't be alone?' We blanched and exchanged a penetrating look. Our souls were laid bare. To hide our embarrassment, we started to kiss the child, and one of those kisses landed somewhere else. That night, with lots of tears and the fury of jealousy, we conceived a little brother for the daughter of the man who stole my happiness."

"What a strange story."

"But our love, if you want to call it that, was arid and silent, composed of fire and rage, with few tender words. My wife—I mean the mother of my children, because she's my only real wife—is an attractive woman, maybe even beautiful, but I never lusted after her despite living together. Even after what I just told you, I never thought that I was deeply in love with her until something happened that convinced me I was. Once, after giving birth—it was the birth of our fourth child—she was so sick, so gravely ill, that I thought she was dying. She'd lost a great deal of blood, she was as white as wax. She couldn't keep her eyes open, and I thought I was losing her. I went mad. My face was as white as wax too, the blood froze in my veins. I withdrew to a corner of the house, where no one could see me, and I knelt down and asked God to kill me rather than let this saintly woman die. I cried and pinched and scratched my chest until it bled. And I understood how strong the tie was that bound my heart to the heart of the mother of my children. When she started to feel better, once she'd regained consciousness and was out of danger, I put my mouth close to her ear. She was smiling at the newborn baby lying on the bed, and I told her something I'd never said to her before and have never said the same way since. She smiled and smiled, looking up at the ceiling. I put my lips on her lips, wrapped her bare arms around my neck, and my tears fell on her eyes. 'Thank you, Antonio,' she said. 'Thank you for me, for our children, for all our children, for her, for Rita.' Rita is our oldest daughter, the thief's daughter. No, I mean *our* daughter, *my* daughter. The thief has another daughter, with the woman who once called herself my wife. Do you understand now?"

"That, and so much more, Don Antonio."

"So much more?"

"Yes, more. So you have two wives, Don Antonio?"

"No, I have only one. Only one, the mother of my children. The other isn't my wife. I'm not even sure she's the wife of the father of her child."

"But the sadness in your home . . ."

"The law is always sad, Don Augusto. And love is sad, too, if it's born and grows on the grave of another love, like a plant nourished by another plant's decay. Other people's crimes brought us together. Is our union also a crime? They shattered what should never be shattered. Why shouldn't we put it back together?"

"And you never heard more about . . . ?"

"We haven't wanted to. Our Rita is grown up now. One of these days she'll get married. I've given her my name, of course. The law can do as it pleases. She's my daughter, not the thief's. I raised her."

XXII

"So . . ." Augusto asked Victor, "what happened with the Intruder?"

"I never would have believed it. Never. We were at each other's throats up until the day he was born. While he was fighting to come into the world you have no idea the insults my Elena was flinging at me: 'This is all your fault!' 'Get away from me! Get out of my sight! Aren't you ashamed to be here? If I die, it'll be because of you!' 'This is it, never again! Never!' But once he was born, everything changed. It's as if we'd just woken up from a bad dream and were newlyweds again. I've gone blind with happiness, totally blind. The little guy has blinded me. I'm so blind that Elena seems fresher, healthier, younger, and even more voluptuous than ever, even though everyone tells me that she looks terrible, that she's a bag of bones and has aged at least ten years as the result of the pregnancy."

"That reminds me, Victor, of the story of the fireworks maker I heard in Portugal."

"Tell me."

"You know that in Portugal, fireworks, pyrotechnics, is a real art. If you haven't seen Portuguese fireworks, you have no idea what you can do with them. And, my God, they have the craziest names."

"Tell me the story."

"I'm getting to it. In one of the Portuguese villages there was a pyrotechnician who had a gorgeous wife. She was his comfort and his pride and joy. He was madly in love with her, but even more proud of her looks. He loved to make other men green with envy by parading her around, as if to say, 'See this woman? Do you find her attractive? You do? Well, she's mine, all mine. Eat your hearts out!'

"He would gush about her beauty all the time, even claiming that she was the inspiration for his most beautiful fireworks, his pyrotechnic muse. But once, when he was preparing a show—with his ravishing wife by his side as usual for inspiration—the powder caught fire, there was an explosion, and they had to carry both of them away unconscious with severe burns. The wife was burned over most of her face and chest; she was horribly scarred. But he had the good luck to be completely blinded and could never see how disfigured she was. Afterward, he was as proud of her beauty as ever, bragging to everyone as he walked next to her—she led him everywhere—with the same defiant arrogance as before. 'Have you ever seen a more beautiful woman?' he'd ask, and everyone, knowing what had happened, would pity the poor technician and praise his wife."

"Well, wasn't she just as beautiful to him as she was before?" Victor asked.

"Maybe even more beautiful than before, like your wife after giving birth to the Intruder."

"Don't call him that."

"You started it."

"I know, but I don't want anyone else to call him that."

"That happens a lot. A nickname you give somebody sounds different when someone else says it."

"They say no one knows what their own voice really sounds like."

"Or what their face looks like. Speaking for myself, I confess that one of the things that frightens me the most is looking at myself in the mirror when I'm alone and no one can see me. I start to doubt my own existence and to imagine, looking at myself from the outside, that I'm a dream, a fictional character."

"Then stop looking at yourself."

"I can't help it. I'm obsessed with introspection."

"You'll end up like the fakirs who people say contemplate their navels."

"Well, I think that if you don't know your own voice or face, you probably don't know much about anything else that's yours, intimately yours, almost like a part of you."

"Like your wife, for instance," Victor said.

"Exactly. It must be impossible to really know the woman who shares your life and becomes a deep part of you. Do you know what one of our greatest poets, Campoamor, said about marriage?"

"No. What?"

"He said that when a man gets married, if he's really in love, at first he can't touch his wife's body without going crazy and burning with lust. But after a while, he gets used to her, and eventually there's no difference between touching his wife's naked thigh and his own. But, at the same time, if they had to amputate his wife's thigh, it would hurt him as much as losing his own."

"It's true. You have no idea how much I suffered when my wife was giving birth."

"She suffered more."

"Who knows? And now, since she's mine and such an intimate part of me, even though they say she's lost her figure and is unattractive, I haven't noticed it any more than anyone notices they've lost their own figure, or aged, or become less attractive."

"You don't think people realize they've aged or become less attractive?" Augusto asked.

"Not really, even if they say they do. Especially if it happens slowly and steadily. But if it happens all at once . . . As far as feeling yourself age, never. You feel the things around you age or grow younger. That's the only thing I feel now that I have a child. You know what parents say when they point to their children: 'We've aged so much because of them!' I think that watching a child grow is the sweetest and the most agonizing thing in the world. So don't get married, Augusto, not if you want to enjoy the illusion of eternal youth."

"What am I going to do if I don't get married? How am I going to pass the time?"

"Become a philosopher."

"Isn't marriage the best, maybe the only, school of philosophy?"

"Of course not. Haven't you ever noticed how many of the great philosophers were bachelors? Off the top of my head, apart from those who were monks, there's Descartes, Pascal, Spinoza, Kant . . ."

"Don't talk to me about bachelor philosophers."

"What about Socrates? Don't you remember how he sent his wife, Xanthippe, away on the day he was supposed to die so that she wouldn't upset him?"

"I don't want to hear about that either. I refuse to believe that Plato's story is anything but a novel—"

"Or a nivola . . ."

"If you insist."

Augusto suddenly put an end to this enjoyable conversation and left. A beggar approached him on the street.

"Have pity, for God's sake, I have seven children."

"You shouldn't have had them," Augusto said, annoyed.

"I wish you could have been in my shoes," said the beggar. "What would you have us poor people do, if we don't have children . . . for the rich?"

"You're right," Augusto said, "and since you're a philosopher, here, take this." He gave him a *peseta,* and the good man left immediately to spend it at the nearest tavern.

XXIII

Poor Augusto was distraught. Not only did he find himself caught between Eugenia and Rosario, like Buridan's donkey, but also the tendency to fall in love with every woman he saw was getting worse. He saw signs of it everywhere he looked.

"Go away, Liduvina, please! Leave me alone! Go away!" he told his maid.

As soon as she was gone, he put both elbows on the table, lowered his head between his hands, and thought, This is terrible, I seem to be falling in love unconsciously . . . even with Liduvina. Poor Domingo. No doubt about it. Even though she's fifty, she's still good-looking—still pretty curvy—and sometimes when she comes out of the kitchen with the sleeves rolled up on those shapely arms . . . Come on, this is crazy! But that double chin and those folds on her neck . . . This is terrible!

"Come here, Orfeo," he said, picking up the dog. "What do you think I should do? How am I going to resist all of this until I make up my mind and get married? Wait, Orfeo, I have a brilliant idea. I should devote my time to studying these women I'm obsessed with. What do you think of my studying female psychology? That's it! I'll write two monographs; they're very popular now. One will be entitled *Eugenia* and the other *Rosario*, followed by *A Study of Woman*. What do you think, Orfeo?" He decided to consult Antolín S. (i.e., Sánchez) Paparrigópulos, who was immersed at the time in the study of women—fictional women in books, not in real life.

Antolín S. Paparrigópulos was what you'd call a scholar, a young man who was going to bring glory to his country by shedding light on its most neglected achievements. If the name S. Paparrigópulos wasn't yet known among the boisterous youths making a racket to draw attention to themselves, it was because he had the one quality essential to inner strength: patience. Also, he respected most people and himself so much that he postponed speaking in public until he felt prepared enough to be in total command of his subject.

Instead of using newfangled gimmicks to make a flashy temporary name for himself built on others' ignorance, Paparrigópulos aspired, in all his literary endeavors, to as much perfection as humanly possible—always, of course, within the boundaries of reason and good taste. He didn't want to strike a discordant note to make himself heard, but to use his carefully disciplined voice to strengthen the beautiful, truly national, purebred symphony.

S. Paparrigópulos had a clear, wonderfully transparent intelligence, without any cloudiness or imprecision. He thought in pure Castilian, with no trace of horrid northern mists or any taint of decadent Parisian boulevards—pure, clean Castilian. His thoughts were solid and deep, suffused with the soul of the people who nurtured him and to whom he also owed his spirit. Hyperborean mists were fine for men who drank fortified beer, but not in this cloudless Spain with its dazzling sky and wholesome chalky wine from Valdepeñas. Paparrigópulos agreed with the unfortunate Becerro de Bengoa, who after calling Schopenhauer a crackpot, asserted that it wouldn't have occurred to Schopenhauer to say the pessimistic things he did if he had drunk Valdepeñas instead of beer. Bengoa also declared that the cause of neurosis is not minding one's own business, and that the cure for it is donkey feed.

Antolín Paparrigópulos was convinced that the essence of everything was form—more or less internal form—that the universe itself is only a kaleidoscope of interconnected forms. Believing that it is because of their form that the great works live on through the ages, he labored over the language he was going to use in all his works as painstakingly as did the most wonderful Renaissance artists.

Paparrigópulos was strong enough to resist the currents of neo-romantic sentimentality and also the destructive popular obsession with so-called social problems. He was convinced that society's problems can't be solved here on earth—that there will always be rich people and poor people—and that there can be no solution besides the charity of the rich and the resignation of the poor. Therefore he distanced himself from futile arguments and took refuge in the purest region of unsullied art, far from emotional upheavals, where man finds sweet relief from life's disappointments.

Moreover, he despised the idea of a sterile cosmopolitanism, which overwhelms man's spirit with dreams of impotence and exhausting utopias, and idolized his beloved Spain, so maligned and little known by her offspring—this Spain that would provide him with material for all the works that would grant him his future fame.

S. Paparrigópulos dedicated the powerful forces of his mind to researching the private lives of our people—a work as solid as it was selfless—aspiring to nothing less than reviving our past, his great-grandparents' era, for our citizens. Fully aware of the mistakes made by those who simply use their imaginations, he examined and reexamined all kinds of old records to create an unshakable foundation for his scholarly historical research. In his eyes, every event, no matter how insignificant, had precious value.

He knew that we have to learn to see the universe in a drop of water, that a paleontologist can reconstruct an entire animal from a single bone, just as an archaeologist can reconstruct an ancient civilization from the handle of a cauldron. He also recognized that we shouldn't use a microscope to look at the stars or a telescope to look at infusoria—as some humorists did to confuse things. While he acknowledged that an archaeological genius needed only the handle of a cauldron to reconstruct art buried in oblivion, he was modest and didn't consider himself a genius, so he always preferred having two handles to one—the more the better—or, of course, the entire cauldron.

"What's gained in breadth is lost in intensity." That was his motto. Paparrigópulos knew that a highly specialized article or solid monograph could contain an entire philosophy. Above all he believed that the division of labor had wrought miracles, and that enormous scientific progress had been made by the self-sacrificing army of frog pokers, word hunters, date guessers, and droplet inspectors.

What especially captivated his interest were the most difficult and thorny problems related to our literary history, such as Prudentius's birthplace, although lately—supposedly because he'd been turned down in marriage—he was devoting himself to studying Spanish women of past centuries.

You could best perceive and admire the sharpness, good sense, perspicacity, marvelous historical intuition, and critical acuity of S. Paparrigópulos in his most seemingly insignificant articles. His best qualities shone when applied to concrete, living things, not to abstractions and pure theory. You had to see his mind at work. Every essay was a course in inductive logic, a monumental work as admirable as Lyonet's study of the willows' caterpillar—above all, an example of pure devotion to sacred Truth. He shunned ingeniousness as though it were the plague and believed that only by training ourselves to respect divine Truth in the tiniest detail could we pay it its due respect in the bigger picture.

Paparrigópulos was preparing a popular edition of Kalila and Dimna's fables, with an introduction about Indian literature's influence on Spain in the Middle Ages. It's a shame it was never published, because it would have drawn our people away from the bars and distracted them from poisonous doctrines about unrealistic economic reforms. But he was planning two even greater works. One was a history of obscure Spanish writers, those who don't figure in current literary histories or are mentioned only briefly because of the supposed insignificance of their work—an injustice he despised, feared, and hoped to correct. The second was a study of writers whose works have been lost, whom we know only because their names and titles of their works are mentioned elsewhere. He was also about to begin a history of those who had thought about writing but had never gotten around to it.

To improve his projects' success, once he'd feasted on the rich marrow of our national literature, he plunged into foreign works. But he found this to be wearisome. He lacked a facility for foreign languages, and their mastery required an investment of time he needed for higher pursuits. So he resorted to a practice he'd learned from his distinguished teacher. He read the main works of criticism and literary history published in foreign countries—provided, that is, he could find them in French. Once he had a sense of the average opinion expressed by the most reputable critics regarding this or that author, he would peruse the writer's works quickly to satisfy his conscience and feel free to refine the critics' views without compromising his own scrupulous integrity.

It's obvious, then, that S. Paparrigópulos wasn't one of those wandering, erratic young souls who saunter aimlessly through the realms of thought and imagination, occasionally firing off here and there the sparks of a brilliant idea. No. He followed rigorous, well-planned itineraries, with a destination in sight. If none of his accomplishments stood out, it was because they were all at the highest possible level, like a plateau, like our vast sunny Castilian plains rippling with nourishing golden wheat.

If only Providence would provide Spain with more Antolín Sánchez Paparrigópuloses. With their help, we could take possession of our traditional riches and reap profitable returns with them. Paparrigópulos aspired, and aspires—he's still living and continues to prepare his works—to dig into the soil with his critical plow, even if only a half-inch deeper than those who preceded him in the field. He hopes that with new sources of irrigation, the wheat will grow more luxuriantly, producing more grain, that the flour will be richer in quality, and that we Spaniards will nourish ourselves with better and cheaper bread for our souls.

We've said that Paparrigópulos continues to work and prepare his works for publication. It's true. Augusto had heard—through mutual friends—that he was engaged in studying women.

But he hadn't published anything yet . . . or since.

With the goodwill typical of their profession, having caught a glimpse of Paparrigópulos, many scholars are envious of the fame they think he will attain in the future and try to belittle him. One compares him to a fox who erases his tracks with his tail and runs around this way and that to throw off the hunter and prevent anyone from knowing how he got to the chicken. But if Paparrigópulos is guilty of anything, it's that after building his tower, he leaves the scaffolding there for all to see, preventing us from admiring the tower or even seeing it clearly.

One critic disdainfully calls him a commentator, as if commentary weren't a supreme form of art. Another accuses him of translating or adapting ideas taken from foreign works, forgetting that when Paparrigópulos recasts these ideas in a Castilian Spanish so clear, so transparent, and so pure, he makes them Castilian, and his own, the way Father Isla made Lesage's *Gil Blas* his own. Another critic complains that Paparrigópulos relies on his deep faith in the ignorance of those around him, overlooking the fact that faith can move mountains. But the worst injustice inflicted by these bitter criticisms from people he's never harmed . . . the most glaring injustice is obvious when you remember that Paparrigópulos hasn't published anything yet, and that those who are howling and nipping at his heels are judging him only from hearsay to make their voices heard. This remarkable scholar should only be appraised calmly, without the least bit of *nivolesque* drama.

It occurred to Augusto to consult this man, I mean this scholar, because he knew that Paparrigópulos was studying women. Granted, he was studying women in books, where they're less risky, and from the past, where they're also less risky, than women today.

So it was this Antolín Paparrigópulos Augusto went to see for advice—a reclusive scholar, who was too shy to approach real women and therefore preferred to study them in books. No sooner had Augusto explained his plan than the scholar said, "Poor señor Pérez, I sympathize with you. You want to study women? It's a daunting task."

"You're studying them."

"One must sacrifice oneself. Research—obscure, patient, silent research—is my reason for living. But as you know, I'm a humble, a most humble laborer in the field of thought. I gather and organize materials so that those who come after me will make good use of them. Human labor is collective. If it isn't collective, it's not solid or durable."

"What about the works of our greatest geniuses? *The Divine Comedy*, *The Aeneid*, a Shakespearean tragedy, a painting by Velázquez?"

"It's all collective, much more collective than anyone thinks. *The Divine Comedy*, for example, was preceded by a whole series—"

"Yes, I know."

"As for Velázquez . . . By the way, are you familiar with Justi's book about him?"

For Antolín, the main, in fact almost the *only*, value of the greatest works of human imagination lay in inspiring a book of criticism or commentary. The great artists, poets, painters, musicians, historians, and philosophers were born so that a scholar could write their biography or a critic comment on their works. A great writer's sentence lacked value until a scholar quoted it and mentioned the title, edition, and page where it appeared. All his talk about the fellowship of collective work stemmed from envy and helplessness. Paparrigópulos belonged to the same group of commentators as those Homeric scholars who, if Homer himself reappeared and entered their office chanting his works, would shoo him out the door because he was interrupting their search for a word that occurred only once in the dead language of his texts.

"Tell me, what do you think of female psychology?" Augusto asked.

"Such a vague, generic, abstract question makes no sense to a modest researcher like myself, my friend, a man who isn't and has no desire to be a genius."

"You have no desire to be a genius?"

"That's right. It's an unfortunate thing to be. So your question is too imprecise. Answering it would require—"

"Of course, like your colleague who wrote a book on Spanish psychology. Although he was Spanish and lived among Spaniards, all he did was quote the theories of this man and that and write a bibliography."

"Ah, the bibliography! Yes, I know."

"Never mind, Paparrigópulos. Tell me, as precisely as you can, what you know about female psychology."

"You have to start with an initial question: 'Do women have souls?' "

"Oh, please!"

"You shouldn't be so dismissive, so absolute."

Does *he* have a soul? Augusto wondered. Then he said, "What do you think they have instead of a soul?"

"Do you promise not to divulge what I'm about to tell you, my friend? Although . . . never mind, you're not a scholar."

"What do you mean by that?"

"You're not one of those people who steal the last thing they heard and pretend they came up with it themselves."

"People do that?"

"Oh, my dear Pérez. Scholars are petty thieves by nature. I admit it and I'm a scholar. We go around stealing the little things we discover from one another and trying to keep others from stealing them first."

"That makes sense. The owner of a warehouse protects his goods more carefully than the owner of a factory. You've got to protect the water in a well more vigilantly than the water in a spring."

"Maybe so. All right, since you're not a scholar, if you promise not to reveal my findings before I do, I'll tell you that I've discovered a very interesting theory about the female soul in the writings of an obscure seventeenth-century Dutch writer."

"Let's hear it."

"He says, in Latin, that while every man has his own soul, women have only a single collective soul, something like Averroes's 'active intellect,' which they all share. He adds that they only feel, think, and love in different ways because of physical discrepancies caused by race, climate, nutrition, and so on. That's why these differences are so insignificant. This writer claims that women are much more alike than men, because they're really one and the same."

"That's why, my dear Paparrigópulos, as soon as I fell in love with one, I immediately felt I was in love with all of them," Augusto said.

"Of course. And then this fascinating—but little known—gyne-cologist adds that women have much more individuality than men but much less personality. Every woman feels that she is more unique, more distinct than any man, but with much less inner substance."

"I think I understand what he means."

"That's why it doesn't matter, my friend, if you study one woman or many. The point is to delve deeply into the subject at hand."

"Wouldn't it be better to research two or more and do a comparative study? Comparative studies are very popular these days."

"True. Science and comparison are one and the same. But it's unnecessary when dealing with women. If you know one well, you know them all. You know Woman. Besides, as you know, 'What's gained in breadth is lost in intensity.' "

"True, and I want to study women intensively, not extensively. But at least two . . . two at the very least."

"No, not two. Never. If you're not content with one, which I think is best and enough work as it is, then at least three. Duality is inconclusive."

"Why is duality inconclusive?"

"It's obvious. Two lines can't enclose a space. The simplest polygon is a triangle. So you need at least three."

"But triangles have no depth. The simplest polyhedron is a tetrahedron, so that means at least four."

"In any case, never two. If it has to be more than one, then at least three. But you should study one deeply."

"That's what I plan to do."

XXIV

On the way home from his meeting with Paparrigópulos Augusto was pensive. It looks like I'll have to give up one of them or look for a third, he thought. Although, for a psychological study, Liduvina can represent the third woman, purely as an ideal frame of reference. So I have three: Eugenia, who speaks to my imagination, to my head, Rosario, who speaks to my heart, and Liduvina, my cook, who speaks to my stomach. Head, heart, and stomach are the soul's three components, which some call intelligence, emotion, and will. We think with our heads, feel with our hearts, and desire with our stomachs. That's obvious. And now . . .

Now, he continued, a truly brilliant idea. I'll pretend that I'm interested in Eugenia again and see if she'll accept me as her fiancé and future husband. But only to test her, as a psychological experiment. I'm sure she'll reject me. Of course, she *has* to reject me. After what happened and what she said the last time we met, she'd never get involved with me now. She seems like a woman who keeps her word. Do women keep their word? Does a woman, I mean Woman with a capital *W*, the one Woman spread out among millions of more or less—more rather than less—beautiful female bodies . . . does Woman keep her word? Maybe keeping your word is a masculine trait. No. Eugenia has to reject me, she doesn't love me. She doesn't love me and she's already accepted my gift. If she accepted and is already enjoying its benefits, why should she love me?

But what if she goes back on her word and accepts me as her fiancé and future husband? he thought later. I should consider all possibilities. What if she agrees? That'll be the end of me. I'll have shot myself in the foot, brought this mess on myself. No, that's impossible. But what if she does? Then I'll have to give in. Give in? Yes, give in. Sometimes you have to give in to good luck. Maybe giving in to happiness is one of the toughest lessons to learn. Doesn't Pindar tell us that all of Tantalus's problems come from his inability to be happy? We have to learn to internalize happiness. If Eugenia says yes, if she accepts me, then . . . psychology wins. Long live psychology! But no, she won't agree. She can't, she has to get her own way. You can't twist the arm of a woman like Eugenia. When Woman confronts Man in a battle of wills, to see whose is stronger and more determined, she's capable of doing anything. No, she'll never agree.

"Rosarito is waiting to see you."

With these few emotionally charged words, Liduvina interrupted his thoughts.

"Tell me, Liduvina," Augusto said, "do you think women keep their word? Are you as good as your word?"

"It depends."

"That's what your husband always says. Give me a straight answer, not the kind women usually give. You hardly ever answer the question you're asked, only what you thought you were going to be asked."

"What was it you wanted to know?"

"Whether or not women keep their word."

"It depends on the word."

"What do you mean it depends on the word?"

"Sure, some words are meant to be kept and others aren't. Nobody's fooled, everybody understands what they are."

"All right. Tell Rosario to come in."

As soon as she entered the room, Augusto said, "Tell me, Rosario, do you think a woman should keep her word?"

"I don't recall giving you my word about anything."

"I'm not saying you did. Should a woman keep her word?"

"Oh, I see. It's because of that other . . . because of that woman."

"Whatever the reason. What do you think?"

"I don't understand these sorts of things."

"It doesn't matter."

"Well, if you insist, it's better never to give your word."

"What if you already have?"

"You shouldn't have."

There's no way this girl's ever going to budge, Augusto thought. But now that she's here, I'll carry out a psychological experiment.

"Come, sit down," he pointed to his lap.

The girl obeyed calmly, unperturbed, as if they'd planned and agreed upon this all along. But Augusto was confused and didn't know where to start his psychological experiment. Since he didn't know what to say, well . . . he acted. He hugged Rosario tightly against his chest and covered her face with kisses. I'm afraid I'm going to lose the sangfroid necessary for psychological research, he thought.

He stopped suddenly, seemed to regain his composure, relaxed his hold on Rosario, and blurted out, "Don't you know I'm in love with another woman?"

Rosario was silent. She stared at him and shrugged her shoulders.

"Don't you know that?" he said.

"Why should I care about that now?"

"You don't care?"

"Not right now. Right now I think you love me."

"I think so, too, but—"

Then something strange happened, something Augusto hadn't foreseen or planned for in his psychological experiments on Woman. Rosario wrapped her arms around his neck and started to kiss him. The poor man barely had time to think. Great, now I'm the guinea pig. This girl is studying male psychology. Unaware of what he was doing, he suddenly realized his hands were shaking and that he was stroking the calves of her legs. He sprang from the chair, picked up Rosario, and threw her on the sofa. Her face was flushed but she didn't try to stop him. He pinned down her arms with both hands and looked into her eyes.

"Don't close your eyes, Rosario, please don't. Open them. That's it, a little more. Let me see myself in them. I look so tiny." When he saw himself in her eyes as if in a live mirror, he felt his initial excitement begin to fade.

"Let me see myself in your eyes like I do in a mirror. Let me see a tiny me. It's the only way I'll get to know myself—in a woman's eyes." The mirror was looking at him strangely. This man doesn't seem like the others, Rosario thought. He must be crazy.

Augusto pulled away quickly. He looked down at his body, patted it, and said, "I'm sorry, Rosario."

"Sorry? For what?"

There was more fear than anything else in Rosario's voice. She wanted to run away. When somebody starts to talk and act strangely like this, she thought, anything can happen. This man could kill me in a fit of madness. Tears welled up in her eyes.

"You see?" Augusto said. "Do you see? I'm sorry, Rosario, I'm so sorry. I didn't know what I was doing."

What he doesn't know is what he shouldn't do, she thought.

"Now, go! Go!"

"You're throwing me out?"

"No, I'm protecting myself. I'm not throwing you out, no. God help me. If you'd rather, I'll leave and you can stay here, to prove that I'm not throwing you out."

He's definitely not well, she thought, feeling sorry for him.

"Go now, but don't forget me, all right?" He stroked her chin softly. "Don't forget me. Don't forget poor Augusto." He hugged her and gave her a long hard kiss on the lips. As she was leaving, Rosario turned around and looked back. She seemed oddly fearful. As soon as she left, Augusto thought, She hates me. No doubt about it. I've acted like a fool, a complete and utter fool. But what does the poor thing know about these things? What does she know about psychology?

If Augusto had been able to read Rosario's mind at that moment, he would have been even more distraught. The simple ingenuous girl was thinking, It'll be a cold day in hell before I put myself through something like that again for that other woman.

Augusto was beginning to get agitated again. He realized there was no time to lose—most opportunities knock only once—and became furious with himself. Barely aware of what he was doing, to kill some time, he called Liduvina. When he saw her, so calm, so plump, smiling so impishly, he was overwhelmed with such strange, powerful feelings that he immediately said, "Go away, go!" and left the house. For a moment he was afraid he wouldn't be able to control himself and would pounce on Liduvina.

Once on the street he calmed down. Crowds are like a forest. They put you in your place, ground you. Am I losing my mind? he wondered. Maybe when I think I'm walking down the street like any normal person—what is a normal person anyway?—I'm gesticulating strangely, twisting my body and miming. The people passing by who seem oblivious or indifferent to me might be staring at me, laughing or pitying me. Does the fact that I'm thinking this mean that I'm insane? Can I really be crazy? In the final analysis, even if I am, so what? If a man with a heart, a good, kind man, doesn't go crazy, then he's a complete bastard. If you're not insane, you're either an idiot or a bastard, which doesn't mean that idiots and bastards don't go crazy too.

What I did to Rosario, he thought, was simply ridiculous. God knows what she thought of me. Why should I care what a girl like that thinks? Poor thing. She responded so innocently. She's just a physical being—purely physical, with no psychological dimension. There's no point in using her as a guinea pig or a frog in psychological experiments. Maybe in physiological ones. Is psychology, especially female psychology, anything more than physiology or, at most, physiological psychology? Do women have souls? I don't have the technical skills to run psychophysiological experiments. I never took any lab courses and I have no equipment. You need equipment to do psychophysiological experiments. So, am I crazy?

After venting these thoughts in the middle of bustling crowds that couldn't care less about his problems, Augusto felt calm again and headed home.

XXV

Augusto went to see Victor, to hold the son who'd arrived late in his life, enjoy the renewed happiness in his home, and consult his friend about his own mental state. When he found himself alone with Victor, he said, "What about that novel . . . what did you call it? Ah, yes, the nivola you were writing? I suppose that now, because of the birth of your son, you've given it up."

"Well, you're wrong. Exactly because of that, because I've become a father, I've started to write again. I fill it with all my joy."

"Would you like to read me some of it?"

Victor brought out the manuscript and began to read passages to his friend.

"Wow, you've really changed," Augusto said.

"Why?"

"There are things in there that verge on being pornographic and even cross the line."

"Pornographic? Not at all. Some of it's crude, but not pornographic. There's an occasional nude, but no nakedness. What there is, is realism."

"Sure, realism, and also . . ."

"Cynicism, right?"

"Yes, cynicism."

"Cynicism isn't pornographic. Crudeness is a way to stimulate the imagination and encourage it to analyze reality on a deeper level. The crudeness is pedagogical. Seriously, it's pedagogical."

"And kind of grotesque."

"You're right, I admit it. I like buffoonery."

"Which is always rather creepy."

"That's why I like it. I like only morbid jokes, black humor. Laughter for its own sake disgusts me, even scares me. Laughter simply prepares us for tragedy."

"Well, I find crude humor really offensive."

"Because you're a loner, Augusto. Do you understand? I write these things as an antidote for . . . No, there's no purpose, they're just fun to write, and if people find them entertaining, that's good enough for me. And if at the same time I help someone like you, someone who's alone in more ways than one . . ."

"What do you mean, in more ways than one?"

"Physically and spiritually."

"Speaking of which, Victor . . ."

"I know what you're going to say. You want to talk about your mental state, which for some time has been disturbing, really disturbing, right?"

"That's right."

"I thought so. Well, then, Augusto, get married. Get married right away."

"But . . . which one should I marry?"

"Ah, so there's more than one."

"How do you know?"

"That's easy. If you'd asked, 'With whom?' I wouldn't have guessed there was more than one, or even anyone in particular. But when you asked, 'Which one should I marry?' you're asking which one of two, or three, or ten, or x number of women."

"Of course."

"So marry any one of the x number you're in love with, the one that's most accessible. Don't give it too much thought. You know, I married without giving it any thought. They made us get married."

"But I've just begun to conduct experiments in feminine psychology."

"The only real experimental study of female psychology is marriage. No one who isn't married will ever be able to conduct psychological experiments on Woman's soul. Marriage is the only laboratory for feminine psychology, or gynopsychology."

"But there's no way out of marriage."

"There's no way out of any real experimentation. Anybody who wants to run an experiment with a way out, without burning bridges, will never attain any real knowledge. Never trust a surgeon who hasn't amputated one of his own limbs, or put yourself in the hands of a psychologist who isn't insane. So get married if you want to understand psychology."

"So then, bachelors . . ."

"Bachelors have no psychology. It's only metaphysics. I mean, something beyond physics, beyond nature."

"What's that?"

"It's where you find yourself right now."

"I'm in a metaphysical realm? But Victor, I'm not beyond nature, I'm on this side of it."

"It's all the same."

"What do you mean, it's all the same?"

"Being on this side of nature is the same as being on that side of it, just as being on this side of space is the same as being on that side of it. See this line?" He drew a line on a piece of paper. "Extend it to infinity in both directions and the ends will meet. They'll come together in infinity, where everything meets and comes together. Every straight line is the curve of a circumference, with an infinite radius, that comes together in infinity. So being on this side of nature is the same as being on that side of it. Isn't that clear?"

"No, it's obscure, really obscure."

"Well, exactly because it's so obscure, you should get married."

"Yes, but I have so many doubts."

"All the better, my little Hamlet. You doubt, therefore you think. You think, therefore you are."

"Yes, to doubt is to think."

"And to think is to doubt, just to doubt. We believe, we know, and we imagine without doubt. Neither faith, knowledge, or imagination presupposes doubt. Doubt even destroys them.

"But we can't think without doubting. It's doubt that converts faith and knowledge—which are somewhat static, inert, and dead—into thought, which is dynamic, restless, and alive."

"What about imagination?"

"Actually, there is some room for doubt there. I usually question what I'm going to have the characters of my nivola say and do. Even after I've had them say or do something, I doubt whether it was the right thing to do, whether it's faithful to who they are. But I move on. So yes, in imagination, which is a kind of thought, there is room for doubt."

While Augusto and Victor were having this nivolesque conversation, I, the author of this nivola that you, my reader, are holding and reading, was smiling enigmatically to myself, watching my nivolesque characters plead my case and justify my methods. I thought, These poor fellows have no idea that they're justifying exactly what I'm doing with them. Similarly, when we look for reasons to justify ourselves, we are trying to justify God. And I'm the God of these two poor nivolesque creatures.

XXVI

Augusto headed toward Eugenia's house prepared to carry out his last psychological experiment, the definitive one, even though he was afraid she'd reject him. He ran into her on the stairs. She was leaving just as he was going up to her apartment.

"You here, Don Augusto?" she said.

"Yes, it's me. But since you're going out, I'll come back another day."

"No, my uncle is upstairs."

"I didn't come to see your uncle. I came to talk to you, Eugenia. I'll come back another day."

"No, let's go up. It's best to strike while the iron is hot."

"But if your uncle's home . . ."

"He's an anarchist. We'll leave him out of it."

She convinced him to go up. Poor Augusto, who'd fancied himself a scientist about to conduct an experiment, now felt like a frog.

When they were alone in the drawing room, Eugenia—still dressed in her street clothes and without removing her hat—said, "All right, let's hear what you have to say."

"Well . . . well . . ." poor Augusto stammered. "Well . . ."

"Well what?"

"I'm a nervous wreck, Eugenia. I've gone over what we said to each other the last time we talked a thousand times. In spite of everything, I just can't accept it. I can't."

"Accept what?"

"Well, this, Eugenia."

"What's this?"

"This. Just being friends."

"Just friends? Don't you value our friendship, Don Augusto? Would you rather be less than friends?"

"No, Eugenia, that's not it."

"Well, then, what?"

"Please don't make it so hard on me."

"You're making it hard on yourself."

"I can't accept it."

"Well, what is it you want?"

"I want . . . I want us to get married."

"Let's put an end to that once and for all."

"How can it end if it never began?"

"Didn't you give me your word?"

"I didn't know what I was saying."

"What about that girl Rosario?"

"Please, Eugenia, don't bring her up. Forget about Rosario."

Eugenia took off her hat and put it on the coffee table. She sat down again and said, slowly and solemnly, "All right, Augusto. Since you, a man, don't think you have to keep your word, I, who am only a woman, don't have to keep mine either. Besides, I want to free you from Rosario and the other Rosarios or Petras who might entrap you. What gratitude for your generosity couldn't do, or bitterness because of what happened to me with Mauricio—you see how open I am with you—compassion has been able to achieve. It's true. I feel sorry for you, Augusto, very sorry." As she said this, she patted his knee gently with her right hand.

"Eugenia!" He held out his arms to embrace her.

"Careful!" She pulled back, out of reach. "Easy now!"

"But the other time, last time . . ."

"Yes, but that was different."

I've become the frog, thought the experimental psychologist.

"That's right," Eugenia said. "A girl can allow a friend who's just a friend to be a little more forward than . . . well . . . a fiancé."

"I don't understand."

"I'll explain it to you once we're married. But for now, keep your hands to yourself."

I'm doomed, thought Augusto, who now felt totally and completely like a frog.

"Now," Eugenia said, standing, "I'm going to call my uncle."

"What for?"

"What do you think? To tell him our news."

"Of course," Augusto said, flustered.

Don Fermín soon entered the room.

"Look, *tío*," Eugenia said. "Here's Don Augusto Pérez, who's asked me to marry him. And I said yes."

"Amazing, amazing!" said Don Fermín. "It's amazing. Come here, child, let me give you a hug. Amazing!"

"Is it so amazing that we're going to get married, *tío*?"

"No, what amazes me . . . what astonishes me and knocks me off my feet is the way the two of you have managed this alone, without any help from anyone. Hurray for anarchy! It's too bad you need some kind of authority to make it official. Not in your innermost conscience, of course. The ceremony is merely pro forma, that's all, just pro forma. I know you already consider yourselves husband and wife. In any case, I and I alone, in the name of an anarchical God, hereby marry you. And that's good enough. Amazing! Amazing! Don Augusto, from this day forward, consider this your home."

"From this day forward?"

"You're right, it's always been your home. My house . . . mine? This house I live in has always been yours, it belongs to all my brothers. But starting today . . . you understand."

"Yes, he understands what you mean, *tío*," Eugenia said.

There was a knock at the door and Eugenia exclaimed, "My aunt!" When Doña Ermelinda came in, she looked around and said, "I see. So, it's all settled then? I knew it would be."

Augusto thought, A frog, a complete and utter frog! Together they've all fished me out of the water.

"You'll stay for lunch, of course, to celebrate," Doña Ermelinda said.

"What choice do I have?" the poor frog let slip.

XXVII

Augusto began a new life. He spent nearly every day at his fiancée's house studying not psychology but aesthetics.

And Rosario? Rosario never returned to his home. The next time, another woman delivered his laundry. He didn't dare ask why Rosario didn't come. There was no point, he could guess the reason. He understood her disdain, and it was clearly disdain. Instead of being upset by it, he found it almost amusing. Eugenia would more than compensate for it. But, of course, his future wife kept saying, "Keep those hands to yourself!" She wouldn't give an inch.

Eugenia would only let him look at her, that's all, which only made him hunger for her more. Once he said to her, "I'd love to write a poem about your eyes."

"Go ahead," she replied.

"It would help if you'd play a little piano. Hearing you play your instrument would inspire me."

"You know that your generosity allowed me to stop giving lessons. I haven't touched the piano since. I hate it, Augusto, it's made my life miserable."

"Never mind. Play it, Eugenia. Play it to help me write my poem."

"All right, just this once."

Eugenia sat down at the piano and while she was playing, Augusto wrote the following:

My soul wandered far from my body,
lost in the mists of idea.
Lost there, among the musical notes
they say are sung by the spheres.
My body was alone,
wandering soulless and sad
throughout the earth.
Born to plow through life together,
they didn't really live,
for he was only matter,

and she no more than spirit seeking completeness.
Sweet Eugenia!
But your eyes burst forth like fountains
of vivid light along my path.
And they captured my soul
and brought it from a vague heaven
to a dubious earth.
They placed it in my body,
and since then, and only since then,
have I been alive, Eugenia!
Your eyes are like fiery nails
that join my body to my spirit.
They cause my blood to dream feverishly
and transform my ideas into flesh.
If that light of my life were extinguished,
severing spirit from matter,
I would be lost in the mists of heaven
and the depths of voracious night.

"What do you think?" Augusto said, after reading it to her.

"It's like my piano, it has little or no musicality. And the phrase 'they say' . . ."

"That's to give it a touch of familiarity."

"I think 'sweet Eugenia' is just padding."

"You think you're just padding?"

"In that poem, yes. All of it seems very . . . very . . ."

"I know, very nivolesque."

"What does that mean?"

"Nothing. It's just a joke between me and Victor."

"Look, Augusto, I don't want any in-jokes in my house after we're married. No in-jokes and no dogs. You'd better start thinking about what you're going to do with Orfeo."

"But, Eugenia, for God's sake. I told you how I found the poor little thing. Besides, he's my confidant. He listens to all my monologues."

"There won't be any monologues in my house once we're married. There's no room for a dog. A dog will just get in the way."

"For heaven's sake, Eugenia. At least until we have a child."

"If we have one."

"Of course," Augusto said. "And if we don't, why not a dog? Why not? People say he'd be man's best friend if he had money."

"No, a dog wouldn't be man's best friend if he had money. I'm sure about that. He's his friend because he has none."

Another day, Eugenia approached Augusto. "Listen, I have to talk to you about something serious. I apologize in advance if what I'm about to to say is . . ."

"Please, Eugenia, what is it?"

"You remember my ex-fiancé?"

"Yes, Mauricio."

"You don't know why I had to break up with that cad, but . . ."

"I don't want to know."

"That's to your credit. Well, I had to tell that lazy, good-for-nothing bum to get lost, but . . ."

"He still won't leave you alone?"

"Still."

"If I get my hands on him . . ."

"No, it's nothing like that. He's still chasing after me, but not for the reasons you think. For other reasons."

"Tell me!"

"Don't worry, Augusto. Poor Mauricio's bark is worse than his bite."

"Well, you know the old Arabic proverb: 'He who stops on the road for every dog that barks will never reach his destination.' It's no use throwing rocks at him. Ignore him."

"I think there's a better way."

"What is it?"

"To carry pieces of bread in your pocket and throw it at the dogs who run out and bark at us. They're barking because they're hungry."

"What do you mean?"

"The only thing Mauricio wants now is for you to find him a job or a way to make a living. Then he'll leave me alone. If not . . ."

"If not . . . ?"

"He threatens to come after me and compromise my reputation."

"He's a shameless bastard!"

"Calm down. I think we'd better get rid of him by finding him a job that will support him and take him as far away as possible. I feel kind of sorry for him. The poor guy can't help the way he is and . . ."

"Maybe you're right, Eugenia. Look, I think I can settle all of this. Tomorrow I'll talk to a friend of mine and we'll find him a job."

In fact, Augusto was able to find Mauricio a job, one that would take him far away.

XXVIII

One morning Liduvina announced to Augusto that a young man was waiting to see him. He scowled when he heard it was Mauricio. He was about to send him away without hearing what he had to say, but he was curious about the man who'd been Eugenia's fiancé, the man she'd loved—and maybe still loved in a way—the man who probably knew more intimate things about his future wife than he did, the man who . . . They had a common bond.

Mauricio began humbly. "I've come to thank you, señor. You were kind enough to do me the wonderful favor Eugenia asked you to do."

"There's no need to thank me. I hope that from now on you'll leave my future wife alone."

"I haven't bothered her at all."

"I know what I'm talking about."

"Ever since she broke up with me—she was right, I'm not the best match for her—I've tried to respect her wishes and console myself as best I can. If she's said something to the contrary . . ."

"Please don't talk about my future wife again, especially to insinuate that she hasn't been truthful. Find comfort any way you can and leave us alone."

"Of course. I thank both of you again for getting me this little job. I'm going to accept the position and console myself as best I can. I'm thinking of taking a young lady with me."

"That's none of my business."

"I think you might know her."

"What? Are you making fun of . . . ?"

"No. Her name is Rosarito. She irons clothes at a laundry. I think she used to iron yours and deliver them to you."

Augusto blanched. Does this guy know everything? This bothered him even more than his earlier suspicion that Mauricio knew things about Eugenia that he didn't know.

He recovered right away and said, "Why are you bringing this up now?"

"I think," Mauricio said, as if he hadn't heard Augusto, "that those of us who've been rejected should be allowed to console each other."

"What do you mean? Tell me what you mean." Augusto was considering whether he should strangle the guy here, the scene of his last encounter with Rosario.

"Don't get so worked up, Don Augusto. I'm not insinuating anything. The woman you don't want me to mention snubbed and rejected me, and I met this poor girl who'd been rejected by someone else and . . ."

Augusto couldn't contain himself any longer. His face turned white, then red. He stood up, and almost unaware of what he was doing, he grabbed Mauricio by the arms, lifted him off the floor, and threw him on the sofa as if he were going to strangle him.

When Mauricio found himself on the sofa, he said coldly, "Take a look at yourself now, Don Augusto, in the pupils of my eyes. See how tiny you look."

Poor Augusto felt as if he were melting away. He felt the strength drain out of his arms, and the room began to dissolve into a fog. Could this be a dream? Then he saw Mauricio standing in front of him, staring at him with a cunning smile.

"It was nothing, Don Augusto. I'm sorry. I lost my mind for a moment. I didn't know what I was doing, I didn't realize . . . Thank you, thanks again. My thanks to you and to . . . her. Good-bye."

As soon as Mauricio left, Augusto called Liduvina.

"Tell me, Liduvina, who was just here with me?"

"A young man."

"What did he look like?"

"Do you honestly need me to tell you?"

"Was someone really here with me?"

"Señor!"

"No. Swear to me that a young man was here with me and tell me what he looked like. Tall and blond, right? With a moustache, more stocky than thin, with a pointy nose? Was he here?"

"Are you all right, Don Augusto?"

"It wasn't a dream?"

"Not unless we both dreamed it."

"No, two people can't have the same dream at the same time. That's how we know something isn't a dream, because more than one person experiences it."

"Of course, calm down. The young man you're talking about was here."

"What did he say when he left?"

"He didn't say anything to me when he left. I didn't even see him."

"Do you know who he is, Liduvina?"

"Yes, I know who he is. He was engaged to . . ."

"That's enough. Who's he seeing now?"

"That I can't possibly know."

"Yet you women know so many things without being taught."

"On the other hand, the things people want to teach us don't seem to sink in."

"All right. Tell me the truth, Liduvina. Do you know who this . . . guy is seeing now?"

"No, but I can guess."

"How?"

"From everything you're saying?"

"All right, tell Domingo to come here."

"What for?"

"I want to know if I'm still dreaming, and if you're really Liduvina, his wife, or—"

"Or whether Domingo is dreaming too? I think there's a better way to find out."

"What's that?"

"Call Orfeo."

"You're right. He never dreams."

A short time after Liduvina left, Orfeo came into the room.

"Come here, Orfeo," his master said. "Come here. Poor thing. There's only a few days left for us to live together. She doesn't want you in the house. Where am I going to take you? What am I going to do with you? What's going to happen to you without me? You could die, I know. Only a dog is capable of dying without its master, and I've been more than a master to you. I've been your father, your god. She doesn't want you in the house, she's driving you away from me. Does she think that you, the very symbol of fidelity, will get in her way? Who knows? Maybe a dog picks up the innermost thoughts of the people he lives with, and even though he keeps them to himself . . . I have to get married. I have no choice but to get married. Otherwise, I'll never escape my dream. I have to wake up.

"Why are you looking at me like that, Orfeo? You look like you're crying without any tears. Do you want to tell me something? I can see that you're suffering because you can't speak. I was so quick to assert that you don't dream. Of course you're dreaming of me, Orfeo. The only reason men are men is because there are dogs and cats, and horses and oxen, and sheep, and all kinds of animals, especially domestic ones. Would men ever have become humane if they hadn't unloaded the bestial part of life onto domestic animals? If men hadn't broken the horse, wouldn't half our race be carrying the other half on its back? We owe our civilization to you. And to women. Or maybe women are just another kind of domestic animal. If there were no women, would men be men? Oh, Orfeo. An outsider is coming to this house who's going to throw you out."

He clutched Orfeo tightly to his chest and the dog—who really seemed to be weeping—licked his chin.

XXIX

All the wedding arrangements had been made. Augusto wanted a small, simple wedding, but his future wife preferred a more extravagant, showy one. As the day approached, the groom ached to take small liberties and be more intimate with her, but Eugenia was becoming even more reserved.

"In a few days you'll be mine and I'll be yours, Eugenia."

"That's exactly why we should start to respect each other now."

"Respect . . . respect? Respect seems to exclude affection."

"That's what you think. Just like a man!"

Augusto noticed something strange and unnatural in Eugenia. At times it seemed she avoided his glances. He remembered his poor mother and her undying wish for her son to be happily married. And now, just as he was about to marry Eugenia, he was tormented more than ever by what Mauricio had said about taking Rosario with him. He was wildly jealous and furious because he'd allowed an opportunity to pass and made a fool of himself in front of the young girl.

The two of them are probably laughing at me, he thought, and he's laughing twice as hard because he stuck me with Eugenia and is stealing Rosario away. Sometimes he was tempted to break off his engagement, woo Rosario, and snatch her away from Mauricio.

"Whatever happened to that girl Rosario?" Eugenia asked him a few days before the wedding.

"Why are you bringing her up now?"

"If it bothers you, I won't."

"No . . . but . . ."

"She interrupted us once when we were talking. Have you had any news of her since?" She gave him a piercing look.

"No, I don't know anything about her."

"I wonder who's wooing her or if she has a boyfriend now." She looked away from Augusto and gazed far away into space.

Strange forebodings flashed through the groom's mind. She seems to know something, he thought. And then, out loud, "Have you heard anything about her?"

"Me?" she answered, feigning indifference. She looked at him again. A mysterious shadow floated between them.

"I guess you've forgotten all about her," Eugenia said.

"Why do you keep talking about that girl?"

"I don't know, because . . . Changing the subject, what do you think happens to a man when another man steals the woman he loves and makes off with her?"

Augusto felt the blood rush to his head when he heard this. He had a sudden urge to leave, find Rosario, win her back, bring her to Eugenia, and say, "Here she is. She's mine and not your Mauricio's!"

There were three days left before the wedding. Augusto left his fiancée's house deep in thought. That night he could barely sleep. The next morning, as soon as he woke up, Liduvina came into his room. "A letter came for you just now, señor. I think it's from señorita Eugenia."

"A letter from Eugenia? She sent me a letter? Just leave it and go."

Liduvina left the room. Augusto began to shake. A strange uneasiness made his heart beat faster. He thought about Rosario and then about Mauricio, but he was reluctant to touch the letter. He looked at the envelope fearfully. He got up, washed, got dressed, asked for his breakfast, and devoured it. No, I don't want to read it here, he thought. He left the house and went to the closest church. There, surrounded by a few worshippers hearing mass, he opened the letter. I'll have to control myself here, he thought, because my heart is filled with dread. The letter said:

Dear Augusto: When you read these lines I'll be with Mauricio on our way to the town where he's employed thanks to your kindness. Thanks to you, I'm also able to enjoy income from my property, which, combined with his salary, will allow us to live rather comfortably. I don't ask you to forgive me. I'm sure this will convince you that I could never make you happy, much less you me. Once you've recovered from the initial shock, I'll write again to explain why I'm doing this now and in this way. Mauricio wanted us to leave the same day as the wedding after exiting the church, but his plan was complicated and seemed unnecessarily cruel. As I told you once before, I think you and I can remain friends.

Your friend,
Eugenia Domingo del Arco

P.S. Rosario isn't coming with us. She's staying there and you can console yourself with her.

Augusto collapsed onto a pew, overcome. After a while he knelt down and prayed. When he left the church, he seemed to feel calm, but it was like the terrible calm before a storm. He went to Eugenia's house, where he found her aunt and uncle beside themselves. Their niece had sent them a letter informing them of her decision and hadn't come home that night. She and Mauricio had taken a night train, shortly after Augusto's last conversation with his fiancée.

"What should we do now?" asked Doña Ermelinda.

"What can we do, señora?" Augusto said. "We have to accept it."

"This is an outrage!" said Don Fermín. "Such things shouldn't go unpunished!"

"This, coming from you, Don Fermín? An anarchist?"

"What's that got to do with it? This just isn't done. You should never betray a man like this."

"She didn't betray the other guy," Augusto said coolly, immediately terrified by the iciness with which he'd said it.

"She'll betray him, too . . . she will. You can be sure of it."

Augusto felt a diabolical thrill when he thought about Eugenia someday betraying Mauricio. "But not because of me." He muttered this so softly he barely heard himself.

"Well, my friends," he said, "I'm deeply sorry about what's happened, especially because it concerns your niece, but I have to go."

"You understand, Don Augusto, that we . . ." Doña Ermelinda began.

"Of course, of course. But . . ." Augusto couldn't stay any longer. After exchanging a few more words, he left.

He was afraid of himself and of what was happening to him, or rather, what wasn't happening. The apparent coolness with which he'd reacted to this terrible deceit, his composure, made him doubt his very existence. If I were a man like other men, he thought, a man with a heart . . . If I were even a man at all, if I really existed, how could I have reacted so calmly to this? He began to pat his body instinctively, even to pinch himself, to see if he felt anything.

Suddenly he felt something tugging at his leg. It was Orfeo, who'd come out to greet and console him. As soon as he saw Orfeo, he felt strangely elated. He picked him up and said, "Cheer up, my Orfeo, cheer up. Let's both cheer up. Now you won't be thrown out of the house. No one will take you away from me; no one will keep us apart. We'll live together in life and in death. Every cloud has a silver lining, no matter how big the cloud is, or how thin the lining, or vice versa. You . . . you're truly faithful, Orfeo. I'm sure that occasionally you'll want to mate, but you won't run away from home, you won't abandon me. You're faithful. And listen, I'll bring a female dog to live here so you won't ever have to leave me. I will. Did you run out to meet me to console me for the pain I must be feeling, or are you returning from a visit to your bitch? Anyway, you're faithful, and now nobody's going to throw you out. No one's going to separate us."

He went into his home. But as soon as he found himself inside and alone, the storm, which had seemed so calm, erupted. A flood of emotions swept through him, mixing sadness—bitter sadness—jealousy, rage, fear, hatred, love, compassion, scorn, and above all, shame, deep shame, and the terrible awareness that he'd been made a fool.

"She killed me," he told Liduvina.

"Who?"

"Her."

He locked himself in his room. Alongside the images of Eugenia and Mauricio rising up in his mind was the image of Rosario, who also mocked him. He thought of his mother. Augusto threw himself on the bed and stuffed a corner of the pillow in his mouth. He couldn't think of anything to say. There was no monologue. He felt his soul withering away and he burst into tears. He cried and cried and cried, all thoughts dissolving with his silent tears.

XXX

Victor found Augusto slumped in a corner of a sofa, staring down at the floor and beyond.

"What is it?" he said, laying a hand on Augusto's shoulder.

"How can you ask me that? Don't you know what's happened to me?"

"I know what happened. I mean, I know what she did. But I don't know what you're feeling and why you're reacting like this."

"It's unbelievable."

"So love A disappeared. Don't you still have B, C, D, or any one of the x number of others?"

"This is no time for jokes."

"You're wrong. This is the perfect time for jokes."

"Losing her love isn't what hurts the most. It's the ridicule, the ridicule! They've mocked me, humiliated me, made a fool of me. They wanted to show me . . . I don't know . . . that I don't exist."

"Lucky you!"

"Don't tease me, Victor."

"Why shouldn't I tease you? You wanted to conduct an experiment. You wanted to make her the frog, and she made you one instead. So jump in the pond, start croaking, and get on with your life."

"Again, I beg you . . ."

"Not to make jokes? Well, I will. Jokes were made for situations like this."

"Yours are caustic."

"We should be caustic, we should be confusing, especially confusing. We should confuse everything: dreaming with waking, fiction with reality, truth with falsehood—mix everything up in one big fog. Jokes that aren't caustic and confusing are useless. Children laugh at tragedy; old men cry at comedies. You wanted to make her the frog, but she made you one instead. Accept it and be a frog."

"What do you mean?"

"Experiment on yourself."

"You mean commit suicide?"

"I'm not saying yes or no. It would be one solution, but not the best one."

"Then I should track them down and kill them instead."

"Killing for its own sake is senseless—although it might get rid of the hatred that does nothing but corrupt the soul. More than one bitter man has rid himself of resentment and felt pity, even love, for his victim once he released his hatred. Bad deeds can free us from bad feelings. That's because it's the law that creates sin."

"So, what am I going to do?"

"You must have heard that in this world it's eat or be eaten."

"Sure, ridicule or be ridiculed."

"There's a third alternative: ridicule yourself, devour yourself. He who devours enjoys, but he worries so much about his pleasure coming to an end that he becomes a pessimist. He who is devoured suffers, but he focuses so much on the end of his torment that he becomes an optimist. Devour yourself, and since the pleasure of devouring yourself will become confused with and neutralized by the pain of being devoured, you'll reach the state of perfect equanimity—ataraxy. You'll become a mere spectacle for yourself."

"You, Victor? You're talking like this?"

"Yes, Augusto, I am."

"You never used to think in such a . . . corrosive way."

"I wasn't a father then."

"So, being a father . . . ?"

"If you're not crazy or an idiot, being a father awakens the most terrible thing in a man—a sense of responsibility. I bequeath to my son the eternal legacy of humanity. Just thinking about the mystery of paternity is enough to drive me insane. If the majority of fathers don't go crazy, it's because they're stupid . . . or aren't real fathers. You should rejoice, Augusto. In running away, she may have spared you from becoming a father. I told you to get married, not to have children. Marriage is a psychological experiment, but paternity is a pathological one."

"But she *has* made me a father, Victor."

"What? She's made you a father?"

"Yes, to myself. I think I've truly been born now—to suffer, to die."

"Yes, the second birth—the real birth—consists of being born through pain into the awareness of endless death, a recognition that we're always dying. But if you've become a father to yourself, you've also become a son."

"Victor, after all that's happened to me, after what she's done to me, it seems impossible that I can still listen calmly to this banter, these conceptual games, these macabre jokes, and what's worse . . ."

"What?"

"What's worse is that they distract me. I'm furious with myself."

"It's the play, Augusto. It's the play we perform for ourselves in what's called the inner forum, on the stage of our consciousness, where we appear both as actors and spectators. When we're performing a painful scene, portraying pain, it seems illogical to want to burst out laughing. But that's when we feel like laughing the most. It's the comedy, the comedy of pain."

"What if the comedy of pain drives you to suicide?"

"Then it's the comedy of suicide."

"But death is real."

"It's also theater."

"Then what's real or true or deeply felt?"

"Who told you that theater isn't real or true or deeply felt?"

"So?"

"It's all one and the same. You have to mix things up, Augusto, mix everything up. He who doesn't confuse, becomes confused."

"He who confuses, also becomes confused."

"Maybe."

"Then what?"

"Do what we're doing now: shoot the breeze, split hairs, play with words and definitions, have a good time."

"I'm sure *they're* having a good time!"

"You are too. Have you ever found yourself more interesting than you are right now? How do you know you have an arm or a leg unless it hurts?"

"All right, but what am I going to do right now?"

"Do . . . do . . . do! You're already feeling like a character in a play or a novel. Let's content ourselves with being characters in a nivola.

Do . . . do . . . do! Aren't we doing something when we talk like this? We're obsessed with action, or rather, with acting. They say that a play is filled with action when actors make grand gestures, stride across the stage, pretend to have duels and jump around. Acting! Acting! Other times people complain the actors talk too much. As if talk weren't action. In the beginning was the Word, and through the Word everything was created. For instance, if some nivolist hiding here now behind that armoire jotted down everything we're saying and published it, readers would think that nothing was happening, and yet . . ."

"But if they could see inside me, I guarantee they wouldn't say that, Victor."

"Inside? Inside who? You? Me? We have no insides. Of course, readers wouldn't say that nothing is happening here if they could see inside themselves. The soul of a character in a play or a novel, or a nivola, is given to him by . . ."

"By his author."

"No, by the reader."

"I assure you, Victor, that . . ."

"Don't assure me of anything and devour yourself. That's a sure thing."

"I am devouring myself, I am. I started out as a shadow, a fiction. For years I've wandered around like a ghost, like a puppet made out of fog, doubting my own existence, thinking that I was an imaginary character invented by some hidden genius to comfort or unburden himself. But now, after what they've done to me—after what they did to me—after this ridicule, this vicious ridicule, now I can feel myself, I can touch myself, I no longer doubt that I really exist."

"Theater, theater, theater!"

"What?"

"Sure. In a play the man playing the king believes he's a king."

"Why are you saying these things?"

"To distract you. And also so that, as I said, if a hidden nivolist is listening and jotting down our conversation in order to publish it someday, that nivola's reader will doubt, even for a brief moment, his own physical reality and think that he, too, might be a nivolesque character just like us."

"Why?"

"To free him."

"Yes, I've heard people say that the most liberating thing about art is that it makes you forget you exist. People immerse themselves in novels to distract themselves and forget their problems."

"No, the most liberating thing about art is that it makes you doubt you exist."

"And what does it mean to exist?"

"You see? You're beginning to recover. You're starting to devour yourself. The proof is in the question 'To be or not to be?' that Hamlet—one of those guys who invented Shakespeare—asks."

"Well, to me, Victor, 'To be or not to be?' has always seemed vacuous."

"The more profound a saying is, the more vacuous. There's nothing deeper than a bottomless well. What do you think is the truest truth?"

"Well . . . what Descartes said: 'I think, therefore I am.' "

"No. It's this: *A* equals *A*."

"But that's meaningless."

"That's why it's true, because it has no meaning. And as far as Descartes's ridiculous statement, do you think it's indisputable?"

"Absolutely."

"Didn't Descartes say it?"

"Yes."

"Then it wasn't true. Since Descartes was only a fictitious character himself, invented by history, he didn't exist . . . nor did he think."

"Who said that?"

"Nobody. It said itself."

"So . . . the thing that existed and thought was the thought itself?"

"Of course! Imagine, it's the same as saying that being is thinking and that whatever doesn't think, can't be."

"Obviously!"

"So, don't think, Augusto, don't think. And if you insist on thinking . . ."

"What?"

"Devour yourself!"

"You mean, commit suicide?"

"That's up to you. Good-bye."

Victor departed, leaving Augusto lost and confused with his thoughts.

XXXI

The storm in Augusto's soul subsided into a terrible calm with the decision to commit suicide. He wanted to destroy himself, the cause of his misery. But, like a drowning sailor who grasps at a flimsy board, he decided to consult me, the author of this story, before ending his life. Augusto had read an essay of mine in which I alluded to suicide, and this, along with some of my other works, had made such an impression on him that he didn't want to leave this world without meeting and talking to me. So he traveled here, to Salamanca, where I've lived for more than twenty years, to pay me a visit.

When they announced his arrival, I smiled enigmatically and asked that he be brought to my study. He entered like a ghost and stared at an oil painting of me watching over the books in my library. I motioned for him to sit down in a chair facing me.

He began by talking about my literary and more or less philosophical works, demonstrating that he knew them quite well—which, of course, flattered me—and then he began to speak about his life and misfortunes. I interrupted him and told him not to bother because I knew as much about the vicissitudes of his life as he did. I proved this to him by relating some of their most intimate details—those he thought most private. He stared at me with genuine terror in his eyes, as if I were a monstrous creature. I thought I saw him blanch and his facial expression change. He even seemed to be trembling. He was spellbound.

"This is incredible," he said, "incredible. If I hadn't seen it, I'd never have believed it. I don't know if I'm awake or dreaming."

"Neither awake nor dreaming," I said.

"I don't understand. Since you seem to know as much about me as I do, maybe you've guessed why I came."

"Yes," I said, "You're"—I said this in my most authoritative tone—"you're feeling overwhelmed by your misfortunes and have conceived the diabolical idea of killing yourself. Before you do, motivated by something you read in one of my essays, you've come to consult me about this decision." The poor man was shaking like a leaf and staring at me as though he were possessed. He tried to stand up, maybe to leave, but he couldn't. He didn't have the strength.

"Don't move," I said.

"It's just . . . it's just . . ." he stammered.

"It's just that you can't commit suicide, even if you want to."

"What?" he said, surprised to be so quickly challenged and rebuffed.

"Yes. What do people need in order to commit suicide?"

"The courage to do it."

"No," I said, "to be alive."

"Of course."

"And you aren't alive."

"What do you mean, I'm not alive? Have I died?" He began to pat his body reflexively.

"No," I said. "I told you before that you're neither awake nor asleep, and I'm telling you now that you're neither dead nor alive."

"For God's sake, explain this to me once and for all," he pleaded, dismayed. "The things I'm seeing and hearing this afternoon are enough to drive me insane!"

"All right. The truth, my dear Augusto"—I spoke in my gentlest voice—"is that you can't kill yourself because you're not alive. You're neither alive nor dead because you don't exist."

"What do you mean, I don't exist?"

"You exist only as a fictional character. You, poor Augusto, are nothing but a product of my imagination and of those who read the fictional adventures and predicaments I've written. You're only a character in my novel, or nivola, or whatever you want to call it. Now you know your secret."

When he heard this, the wretched man could only stare at me with eyes that bore right through me. Then he gazed at the oil portrait of me overlooking my books. His face lost its pallor and he began to breathe more easily. He pulled himself together and regained his composure. Propping both elbows on the table in front of me, Augusto lowered his head between his hands, looked at me with a smile in his eyes, and said slowly, "Listen carefully, Don Miguel, you might be wrong. What's happening may be the opposite of what you think and say."

"What do you mean, the opposite?" I was alarmed to see him come back to life.

"Maybe, my dear Don Miguel, you, not I, are the fictional character who doesn't exist and is neither alive nor dead. Maybe you're just an excuse for my story to be told to the world."

"Let's add insult to injury," I said, irritated.

"No need to get upset, señor de Unamuno. Calm down. You expressed doubts about my existence."

"Not doubts," I interrupted. "I'm absolutely sure that you don't exist outside my novel."

"Well then, don't be annoyed if I doubt your existence instead of mine. Let's settle this once and for all. Haven't you said, not once but many times, that Don Quixote and Sancho are not just as real but even more real than Cervantes?"

"I can't deny it, but what I meant was . . ."

"Never mind, let's forget your intentions and move on," he said. "When a man lying motionless and asleep in his bed dreams something, what exists more, he as a consciousness that dreams or his dream?"

"And what if the dreamer dreams that he exists?" I threw back at him.

"In that case, my friend Don Miguel, I ask you: how does he exist? As a dreamer who dreams of himself or as someone dreamed by him? Also, note that in debating this with me you're acknowledging that I exist independent of you."

"No, I most certainly am not!" I said. "I need to debate. I can't live without debate and contradictions. And when there's no one to debate and contradict me, I invent someone inside me to do it. My monologues are all dialogues."

"Maybe the dialogues you create are nothing more than monologues," Augusto said.

"That may be. But I'm telling you again that you don't exist outside of me."

"And I suggest to you again that perhaps it's you who doesn't exist outside of me and the other characters you think you've invented. I'm sure Don Avito Carrascal and the great Don Fulgencio would agree."

"Don't mention that . . ."

"Fine, don't insult him. Tell me, what do you think about my committing suicide?"

"Well, since you don't exist outside my imagination, and since you ought or are able to do only whatever I damn well please . . . then, since I don't want you to commit suicide, you won't commit suicide. And that's that!"

"To say 'whatever I damn well please,' señor de Unamuno, is very Spanish but extremely rude. Besides, even granting your bizarre theory that I don't really exist and that you do, that I'm nothing but a fictional character, the product of your imagination as a novelist, or a nivolist . . . Even so, there's no reason I should submit to 'whatever you damn well please,' to your every whim. Even fictional characters have their own inner logic."

"Yes, I've heard that before."

"It's true. A novelist or playwright can't do whatever he wants with a character he creates. Artistic rules dictate against fictional characters doing something no reader would expect them to do."

"Characters in a novel perhaps . . ."

"Well, then?"

"But characters in a nivola . . ."

"Let's drop that nonsense," Augusto said. "It's offensive and hurts me deeply. I have my own character, my own way of being, my own inner logic. Whether it's my own, as I believe, or you've given it to me, as you believe, this logic demands that I commit suicide."

"That may be what you think, but you're wrong."

"Let's see. Why am I wrong? How? Show me where I'm wrong. Since self-knowledge is the hardest to acquire, I could be wrong and suicide may not be the most logical solution to my dilemmas, but prove it to me. Because, my friend Don Miguel, if self-knowledge is hard, there's another kind of knowledge that's just as difficult."

"What's that?"

Augusto gazed at me with a wry, enigmatic smile and said slowly, "What's even more difficult than self-knowledge is the idea that a novelist or playwright deeply understands the characters he creates or thinks he creates."

Augusto's comebacks were making me uneasy and I was beginning to lose my patience.

"I insist," he said, "that even if I concede that you created me, a fictional being, you can't prevent me from committing suicide just like that, for no reason, only because you damn well please."

"Enough! That's enough!" I said, banging my fist on the table. "Be quiet! I've had enough of your insolence—and from a creature I created no less. Since I'm fed up and don't know what to do with you, I've decided this very minute that you're not going to commit suicide. I'm going to kill you instead. You're going to die soon, very soon."

"What!" he said, shaken. "You're going to let me die, have me die? You're going to kill me?"

"Yes, I'm going to make you die."

"Never! Never! Never!"

"Ah," I said, looking at him with pity and indignation. "So you were ready to kill yourself, but you don't want me to kill you? You were going to take your own life, but you don't want me to take it?"

"It's not the same."

"You're right. I've heard of similar cases. I once heard of a man who went out one night armed with a revolver intent on taking his own life. Some thieves attacked him and tried to rob him. He defended himself and killed one of them. The others escaped. Seeing that he'd bought his own life with the life of another man, he abandoned his plan."

"That makes sense," Augusto said. "The point was to take a life, to kill a man. After he'd killed someone, why kill himself? Most suicides are failed homicides. Men kill themselves because they lack the courage to kill others."

"I see. I understand what you're saying, Augusto. You mean that if you had the courage to kill Eugenia or Mauricio, or both, you wouldn't be thinking of killing yourself, right?"

"I wasn't thinking of them, exactly . . . no."

"Who, then?"

He looked me in the eyes. "You."

"What!" I said, standing up. "What! You've actually considered killing me? You? Kill me?"

"Sit down and relax, Don Miguel. Do you think it would be the first time a fictional being, as you call me, killed the person he thought had given him a fictional existence?"

"This is too much," I said, pacing around my study. "You've gone too far. This only happens in . . ."

"In nivolas," Augusto said, scornfully.

"All right, enough! Enough! This is unbearable. You come to consult me and begin by questioning my own existence and then my right to do whatever I damn well please with you. Yes, that's right, whatever I damn well please! Whatever I imagine in my . . ."

"Don't be so Spanish, Don Miguel."

"That, on top of everything else, you imbecile? Yes, I'm Spanish! Spanish by birth and education. In body, in spirit, in language, and even by avocation and profession. Spanish above and before all else. Hispanism is my religion, and the heaven I want to believe in is a celestial and eternal Spain. My God is a Spanish God, that of Our Lord Don Quixote, a God who thinks in Spanish and who said in Spanish, 'Let there be light!' and his word was a Spanish word."

"So what?" Augusto interrupted, bringing me back to earth.

"You brought up the idea of killing me. Killing *me*? You? I, die at the hand of one of my creations? I've had enough. To punish you for your audacity, and for the destructive, outrageous, anarchic beliefs you've dared to challenge me with, I hereby resolve and decree that you're going to die. As soon as you return home, you'll die. You'll die, I tell you, you'll die!"

"For God's sake!" begged Augusto, pale and trembling.

"No God can help you now. You're going to die!"

"But I want to live, Don Miguel. I want to live!"

"Weren't you going to kill yourself?"

"If that's the reason, I swear to you, señor de Unamuno, that I won't kill myself. I won't take this life that God, or you, have given me. I swear! Now that you want to kill me, I want to live, to live!"

"Some life!" I said.

"Yes, whatever it may be. I want to live, even if I'm duped again, even if another Eugenia and another Mauricio were to rip my heart to shreds. I want to live, to live!"

"That's no longer possible. It's impossible."

"I want to live, to live . . . and be me, me, me!"

"But you're only what I want you to be."

"I want to be me. I want to live!" His voice was choked with tears.

"It's impossible."

"Listen, Don Miguel, for the sake of your children, for your wife, for whatever is dearest to you. Consider that you'll no longer be you, that you'll die." He fell to his knees, pleading. "Don Miguel, for God's sake, I want to live! I want to be me!"

"It's impossible, my poor Augusto," I said, taking his hand and lifting him up. "It's impossible. I've already written it, there's no turning back. You can't go on living. I don't know what to do with you anymore. When God doesn't know what to do with us, he kills us. And I can't forget that you considered killing me."

"But, Don Miguel, I—"

"It doesn't matter. I know what I'm talking about, and I'm afraid that if I don't kill you soon, you will kill me."

"But didn't we agree that . . . ?"

"It's impossible, Augusto. Your time has come. It's written and I can't turn back. You'll die. Your life can't be worth that much to you anyway."

"For God's sake!"

"There are no 'buts' or Gods that can help you. Go!"

"So it's no?" Augusto asked. "It's no? You won't let me be me and emerge from the fog? Let me live? Let me see me, hear me, touch me, feel my pain, feel me, be me? You refuse? I'm to die a fictional character? Fine, my lord and creator, Don Miguel, you'll die too, you too, and return to the nothingness from which you came. God will stop dreaming you. You'll die. Yes, you'll die, even if you don't want to. You'll die and all those who read my story will die. All of them. Not a single one will be left. They're all fictional characters like me, just like me. All of them, every single one of them will die. I'm telling you this. I, Augusto Pérez, a fictional character just like all of you—nivolesque, just like you. Because you, my creator, Don Miguel, are nothing but another nivolesque character, as are your readers, as am I, Augusto Pérez, your victim."

"Victim?" I exclaimed.

"Victim, yes. You created me to let me die. You'll die, too. He who creates, creates himself, and he who creates himself dies. You'll die, Don Miguel. You'll die, as will everyone who thinks of me. Let's all die then!"

The effort it took to make this passionate plea for life, this hunger for immortality, had worn out poor Augusto. I pushed him toward the door and he left, dejected. He patted himself, as if uncertain of his existence. I wiped away a furtive tear.

XXXII

That same night Augusto left Salamanca, where he'd come to see me. He left with a death sentence weighing on his heart, convinced that it would be impossible to commit suicide even if he tried. Remembering my decision, the poor man tried to delay his trip home as much as possible. But a mysterious attraction, an inner force, drew him on. It was a miserable trip. He rode on the train, counting every minute, literally counting each one: one, two, three, four . . . All his problems, his sad fantasies about loving Eugenia and Rosario, and the tragicomic story of his thwarted marriage had been erased from his memory or, rather, had dissolved into a fog. He could hardly feel the seat he was sitting on. His body seemed weightless. Is it true that I don't really exist? he thought. Is this man right when he says that I'm only a product of his imagination, just a fictional being?

As sad and painful as his life had become, it was even sadder and much more painful to think that it had been nothing but a dream— not even his own dream, but mine. Nonexistence seemed more terrifying than pain. It's one thing to dream that we're alive, but for someone else to dream it . . .

Why shouldn't I exist? he thought. Why? Even if it's true that this man invented me, dreamed me, created me in his imagination, don't I now live in other imaginations, those of the people who read the story of my life? And if I live in the imaginations of many, doesn't that create its own reality? Why then, emerging from the story of my fictitious life, or rather, emerging from the minds of those who read it—of you, who are reading it—why shouldn't I exist as an eternal and eternally wretched soul? Why not?

The poor man couldn't rest. The plains of Castile passed before his eyes, covered with oak trees, with pines. He saw the snowcapped sierras. When he looked back at the faces of the men and women who'd been his companions throughout life's journey, all now enveloped in fog, he felt himself dragged toward death.

He arrived at his apartment, rang the bell, and when Liduvina opened the door, she grew pale at the sight of him.

"What's the matter, Liduvina? You seem frightened."

"Dear God! You look more dead than alive, like something from another world."

"I have come from another world, Liduvina, and I'm going to yet another, and I'm neither dead nor alive."

"Have you lost your mind? Domingo! Domingo!"

"Don't call your husband, Liduvina. I haven't lost my mind. No. And, I repeat, I'm not dead . . . although I'll die soon . . . nor am I alive."

"What on earth do you mean?"

"I mean that I don't exist, Liduvina, I simply don't exist. I'm a fictional being, like a character in a novel."

"That's bookish nonsense. Eat a good, hearty meal, tuck yourself into bed, and don't pay any attention to those crazy ideas."

"Do you think I exist, Liduvina?"

"Come on, forget that malarkey. Have your dinner and go to bed. Tomorrow is another day."

I think therefore I am, thought Augusto. Everything that thinks is, and everything that is thinks. Yes, everything that thinks is. I am, therefore I think.

He didn't want to eat any dinner. It was only out of habit and to placate his faithful servants that he asked for a couple of hard-boiled eggs—something light, nothing more. But as he began to eat he developed a strange hunger, an intense craving for more and more food. He asked for two more eggs and then a steak.

"That's it," said Liduvina. "Eat up. You must be feeling weak, that's all. If you don't eat, you die."

"Even if you eat, you die, Liduvina," Augusto observed sadly.

"Yes, but not of hunger."

"What difference does it make if you die of hunger or of some illness?"

Then he thought, No, I can't die. Only living people die, people who exist. Since I don't exist, I can't die. I'm immortal! There's no immortality like that of someone like me, someone who wasn't born and doesn't exist. A fictional character is an idea and ideas are always immortal.

"I'm immortal! I'm immortal!" Augusto exclaimed.

"What did you say?" Liduvina asked, entering the room again.

"Now bring me . . . what? . . . jellied ham, cold cuts, foie gras, whatever there is. I'm ravenous."

"That's what I like to see, señor. Eat, eat! If you have an appetite, you have a healthy body, and if you have a healthy body, you live."

"But, Liduvina, I'm not living."

"What do you mean?"

"It's obvious. I'm not living. We immortals don't live. I don't live, I *outlive*. I'm an idea."

He began to devour the ham. But if I'm eating, he wondered, how can I not be alive? I eat, therefore I exist. There's no doubt about that. *Edo, ergo sum!* Why do I have this voracious appetite? Then he remembered reading several times that prisoners condemned to death spend their last hours eating in the chapel. I've never been able to understand why, he thought. I do understand the other phenomenon Renan describes in his *L'abbesse de Jouarre*. I can see how a couple condemned to death might feel the urge to make love and reproduce before dying. But to eat? Although . . . of course, it's how the body defends itself. When the soul learns it's about to die, it becomes sad or elated, but the body, if it's a healthy one, develops a ferocious appetite. Because the body knows. My body is defending itself. I eat voraciously, therefore I'm going to die.

"Liduvina, bring me cheese and cookies and fruit."

"It's too much, señor, way too much. It'll make you sick."

"Didn't you just say that if you eat, you live?"

"Yes, but not the way you're eating. You must have heard the saying, 'Food killed more people than Dr. Avicenna cured.' "

"This dinner can't kill me."

"Why not?"

"Because I'm not alive, I don't exist—I already told you."

Liduvina went to get her husband. "Domingo," she said. "I think señor has lost his mind. He's saying strange things—bookish stuff—that he doesn't exist and Lord knows what else."

"What is it, señor?" Domingo said. "Has something happened to you?"

"Oh, Domingo," said Augusto in a voice that sounded otherworldly. "I can't help it. I'm terrified to go to bed."

"Then don't."

"No, I have to. I can barely stand."

"I think you should walk off your dinner. You ate too much."

Augusto tried to stand. "You see, Domingo? You see? I can't even stand up."

"Of course not, you're stuffed."

"Actually, a little ballast helps keep you on your feet. It's that I don't exist. Look, a little while ago, while I was eating dinner, it felt like everything was falling from my mouth into a bottomless barrel. If you eat, you live. Liduvina is right. But if you eat desperately, the way I ate tonight, you don't exist. I don't exist."

"Come on, don't be silly. Drink your coffee and a liqueur to settle your stomach, and let's take a walk. I'll go with you."

"No, I can't stand up. See?"

"You're right."

"Come close and let me lean on you," Augusto told the servant. "I want you to sleep in my room tonight. We'll put down a mattress for you so you can keep an eye on me."

"It would be better for me not to lie down, señor. I can watch over you sitting in an armchair."

"No, I want you to lie down and go to sleep. I want to hear you sleep, or better yet, hear you snore."

"Whatever you say."

"Now listen, bring me a sheet of paper. I'm going to write a telegram that I want you to send as soon as I die."

"But señor!"

"Do as I say."

Domingo obeyed. He brought him paper and ink, and Augusto wrote:

> Salamanca.
> Unamuno.
> You got your way. I died.
> *Augusto Pérez*

"Send this as soon as I'm dead, understand?"

"Whatever you say," replied the servant to avoid arguing more with his master. The two entered the bedroom. Poor Augusto was shaking so hard that he couldn't take off his clothes.

"You undress me," he told Domingo.

"What's the matter, señor? You look like you've seen the devil. You're as white and cold as snow. Do you want me to call the doctor?"

"No, it's no use."

"We'll warm the bed for you."

"What for? Leave it alone. And take off all my clothes. Leave me the way my mother brought me into the world, the way I was when I was born . . . if I was born."

"Don't say that, señor."

"Now put me to bed. Lay me down in the bed. I can't move."

Poor Domingo, who was scared to death, lay his poor master down in the bed.

"And now, Domingo. I want you to recite the Lord's Prayer, the Hail Mary, and the Salve slowly into my ear. That's it, a little at a time, slowly." Then, after repeating them mentally, Augusto said, "Now, listen, take my right hand. Pick it up—it doesn't seem like it's mine anymore, it's as if I'd lost it—and help me cross myself. That's it, that's it. This arm must be dead, see if you can feel my pulse. Now leave me. Let's see if I can sleep a little. But cover me, cover me up well."

"Yes, you should sleep," Domingo said, tucking the blankets around him. "This will pass once you get some sleep."

"Of course this will pass once I get some sleep. But tell me, have I ever done anything but sleep? Anything but dream? Has the whole thing been anything but a fog?"

"Forget all that. That's just book stuff, like my Liduvina says."

"Book stuff . . . book stuff. What isn't book stuff, Domingo? Was there anything before books, before stories, before words, before thoughts? Will there be anything left once thoughts disappear? Book stuff? Who isn't something out of a book? Do you know Don Miguel de Unamuno, Domingo?"

"I've read about him in the newspaper. They say he's a strange man who spends his time spouting off about things that are true but completely irrelevant."

"But do you know him?"

"Me? Why do you ask?"

"Because Unamuno is also book stuff. We all are. And he'll die. Yes, he'll die too, even if he doesn't want to. He'll die, and that'll be my revenge. He refuses to let me live? Well, he'll die too!"

"Well, let the man die in peace when God decides, and get some sleep."

"To sleep . . . to sleep . . . to dream. To die . . . to sleep . . . to sleep, perchance to dream. I think, therefore I am. I am, therefore I think. I don't exist, no, I don't exist. Good Lord! Eugenia . . . Rosario . . . Unamuno . . ." And he fell asleep.

A short time later he sat up in bed, livid, gasping, his eyes black and terrified, looking beyond the darkness, screaming, "Eugenia! Eugenia!" Domingo went to him. Augusto's head dropped onto his chest and he died.

When the doctor arrived he thought that Augusto was still alive. He considered bleeding him and applying mustard plasters, but he soon realized the sad truth. "It was his heart," he said, "asystolic cardiac arrest."

"No, señor," Domingo said. "It was an intestinal blockage. He ate an outrageous amount of food for dinner, which was unlike him. It was unusual for him, as if he wanted . . ."

"To make up for what he wasn't going to eat in the future? Is that it?" the doctor said. "Maybe his heart sensed that he was going to die."

"Well, I think it was a mental problem," Liduvina said. "It's true that he ate a ridiculous amount of food, but he didn't seem to know what he was doing, and he was talking nonsense."

"What kind of nonsense?" the doctor said.

"That he didn't exist, things like that."

"Nonsense?" the doctor muttered, as if talking to himself. Who knows whether or not he existed, least of all him? We know the least about our own existence. We only exist for others. "The heart, the head, and the stomach are all one and the same," the doctor remarked out loud.

"Of course, they're all parts of the body," Domingo said.

"And the body is all one and the same."

"Of course!"

"Even more than you think."

"Do you know how much I think?" Domingo asked.

"You're right. I can see you're not stupid."

"I don't consider myself stupid, doctor, and I don't understand those people who assume everyone is stupid until they prove they're not."

"Well, as I was saying," the doctor continued, "the stomach processes the fluids that form the blood. The heart pumps them to the head and the stomach so that they can function, and the head controls the stomach and the heart's movements. Therefore, señor Don Augusto's body has died in all three areas combined."

"Well, I think," Liduvina said, "that he got it into his head to die, and, of course, if a man is determined to die, well, he dies."

"Absolutely," the doctor said. "If you didn't believe you were going to die, even if you were in the final death throes, you might not die. But as soon as you have the slightest doubt that you can evade death, you're doomed."

"My master's death was a suicide, nothing but a suicide. To eat the way he did after coming home in the state he was in is pure suicide. He got his way."

"Personal problems perhaps."

"Big ones, enormous ones. Women."

"I see. Well, there's nothing we can do now except make the funeral arrangements."

Domingo wept.

XXXIII

When I received the telegram telling me that poor Augusto had died and later learned the circumstances of his death, I wondered if I'd been right to say what I did the afternoon he came to see me about ending his life. I even regretted killing him. I decided he'd been right and that I ought to have let him have his way and commit suicide. I thought about bringing him back to life.

Yes, I'll revive him and let him do whatever he wants, I thought. Let him kill himself if he's determined to do so. I nodded off thinking about bringing him back to life.

Shortly after I fell asleep, Augusto appeared to me in a dream. He was all white, cloud-white, his silhouette illuminated as if by a setting sun. He stared at me and said, "Here I am again."

"Why are you here?" I asked.

"To say good-bye to you, Don Miguel, until eternity, and to order you—not to ask you, to order you—to write a nivola about my adventures."

"It's already written."

"I know, everything is written. I also came to tell you that this idea of reviving me so that I can kill myself is ridiculous. Besides, it's impossible."

"Impossible?" I said. Of course, all of this took place in a dream.

"Yes, impossible. Do you remember the afternoon we met and talked in your study? You were awake, not asleep and dreaming like you are now. I said that, according to you, we fictional creatures have our own inner logic and that our creator can't do whatever he wants with us. Do you remember?"

"Yes, I remember."

"I'm sure that now, despite being so Spanish, you don't feel like doing a damn thing. Do you, Don Miguel?"

"You're right, I don't feel like doing anything."

"No one who's asleep and dreaming feels like doing a damn thing. You and your countrymen sleep and dream. You dream that you want to do something, but you really don't."

"You should be glad I'm asleep," I said. "Otherwise . . ."

"It doesn't matter. As far as bringing me back to life, I must tell you that it's just not feasible. You can't, even if you want to, or dream that you want to."

"Oh, come on!"

"It's true that you can create or kill fictional beings just like those made of what you call real—not fictional—flesh and blood. But once you kill them, you can't revive them. Creating a mortal, carnal, flesh-and-blood man, who breathes air, is easy—too easy, unfortunately. Killing a mortal, carnal, flesh-and-blood man, who breathes air, is also easy—too easy, unfortunately. But bringing him back to life? Bringing him back to life is impossible."

"You're right," I said. "It's not possible."

"The same is true," Augusto said, "exactly the same is true for what you call fictional beings. It's easy—maybe too easy—to give us life. And it's very easy—maybe too easy—to kill us. But to bring us back to life? No one has revived a fictional character who's really died. Do you think it's possible to bring Don Quixote back to life?" he asked.

"Impossible," I said.

"That's true for all of us fictional beings."

"What if I dream you again?"

"No one dreams the same dream twice. That being you'll dream of, who you'll think is me, will be someone else. And now, now that you're asleep and dreaming and know that you're asleep . . . Now that I also know I'm a dream . . . Now I'll repeat what unnerved you so much when I said it before. Look, my dear Don Miguel, it's possible that you are a fictional character who doesn't really exist, neither living nor dead. You may be only an excuse to make my story and others like mine known throughout the world. When you're dead and gone, we may be the ones keeping *your* soul alive. No, don't get upset. You may be asleep and dreaming, but you're still alive. And now, good-bye."

He evaporated into the black fog.

A while later I dreamed I was dying. Just when I dreamed I was taking my last breath, I woke up with a tightness in my chest.

And this is the story of Augusto Pérez.

Funeral Oration as an Epilogue

After a hero or protagonist dies or gets married at the end of a novel, it's customary to explain what happened to the rest of the characters. We're not going to do that here, or relate what happened to Eugenia and Mauricio, Rosario, Liduvina and Domingo, Don Fermín and Doña Ermelinda, Victor and his wife, and all the other characters who've appeared in Augusto's life. We're not even going to describe what they felt or thought about his unusual death. We'll only make one exception, for his dog, Orfeo, who felt Augusto's death the most deeply and sincerely.

Orfeo found himself an orphan. When he jumped on the bed and sniffed his dead master . . . when he smelled his master's death, a thick black cloud enveloped his canine soul. He'd experienced other deaths. He'd smelled and seen dead dogs and cats, he'd killed a few mice, he'd smelled other dead men, but he'd believed his master to be immortal. His master was like a god to him. Now, when he saw that he was dead, he felt the foundations of his faith in life and the world shatter in his soul, and his heart filled with despair.

He curled up at his master's feet. My poor master, he thought. He's dead. He died on me. Everything dies. Everything dies on me. It's worse to have things die on me than for me to die. Poor master. This cold, white thing, lying here, smelling like it's about to go bad—like meat to be eaten—this isn't my master anymore. It's not. Where did my master go, the man who used to pat me and talk to me?

Man is such a strange animal. He ignores what's right in front of him. He strokes our fur for no reason, not when we rub against him, and the more we devote ourselves to him, the more he rejects or punishes us. There's no way of knowing what he wants—if he himself even knows. He always seems distracted, looking at things without really seeing them. It's as if he were living in another world, and clearly, if he's in another world, he's not in this one.

And man speaks, or barks, in such a complicated way. We used to howl, then we learned to bark to imitate him, but even this doesn't really help us comprehend him. We only really understand him when he howls. When man howls, yells, or threatens, we other animals understand him. That's when he doesn't seem preoccupied and in another world. But man barks in his own unique way—he speaks—and that's helped him to invent what doesn't exist and to overlook what does. As soon as he comes up with a name for something, he doesn't see it anymore. He only hears the name he gave it or sees it written down. Language enables him to lie, to invent what doesn't exist and get confused. Everything is an excuse to talk to other men or to himself. He's even infected dogs with this disease.

Man is a sick animal, no doubt about it. He's always sick. He only seems healthy when he's asleep—and not always even then, because he sometimes talks in his sleep. He's infected us with this too. He's infected us with so many things.

On top of it all, he insults us. He uses the word *cynicism*, from the Greek "doggy" or "dogginess," to mean impudence and shameless-ness. He, the most hypocritical of all the animals! If impudence is cynical, or "doglike," then hypocrisy is humanlike!

He's wanted to make dogs hypocrites, too, by turning us into clowns and buffoons. We dogs, who were never forcefully conquered and tamed by him like bulls or horses, but who bonded with him freely, in mutual agreement, to hunt. We sniffed out the game, he hunted it and gave us our share. Our partnership began with a social contract.

And he's rewarded us by debasing and insulting us, wanting to convert us into clowns, monkeys, and "clever dogs." "Clever dogs" are the ones men train to perform in skits. They dress them up and teach them to walk shamelessly on their hind legs. "Clever dogs!" That's what men call cleverness—the ability to prance around on two legs and perform in skits!

Of course, a dog that walks on his hind legs reveals his private parts immodestly, cynically. That's what happened to man when he stood up and turned into an upright mammal. As soon as he did, he felt shame and the moral obligation to cover his private parts. That's why his Bible says . . . so I've heard . . . that the first man to walk on two feet was ashamed to present himself naked before his God. That's why man invented clothes—to cover his sexual organs. But then, since both sexes wore the same clothes, they couldn't tell each other apart. They couldn't always tell what sex they were, and they committed a thousand human atrocities, which they insist on calling "doglike" or "cynical." It's men who have perverted dogs, who've turned us into curs and cynics and made us hypocritical. Cynicism in a dog is hypocritical, just as hypocrisy in a man is cynical. We've infected each other.

At first, men and women wore the same garments, but since they couldn't tell each other apart, they had to invent different clothing to reveal their gender. Pants are the result of man standing on two feet. Man is such a strange animal. His mind is never where it ought to be—that is, where he is. He talks in order to lie, and he wears clothes.

Poor master. Soon they'll bury him in a place set aside for that. Men keep or store their dead, preventing dogs and crows from devouring them. All that remains is what every animal, beginning with man, leaves in this world—a few bones. They store their dead. An animal that talks, wears clothes, and stores its dead. Poor man!

My poor master. He was a man, yes, he was no more than a man. He was only a man, but he was my master. And he owed me so much without even knowing it, so very much. I taught him a lot with my silences, licking his hand while he talked and talked and talked. "Do you understand?" he'd say. And yes, I did. I understood while he talked to himself through me. He talked and talked and talked. When he talked to himself through me, he talked to his inner dog. I kept his cynicism alive. He led a dog's life, a miserable dog's life. And those two played a dirty dog's trick, or rather, a monstrous human trick on him. Mauricio played him a mannish trick and Eugenia played him a womanish one. My poor master!

And now here you are, cold and white, motionless, clothed, yes, but without the ability to speak inwardly or outwardly. You no longer have anything to say to your Orfeo, and Orfeo, with his silence, no longer has anything to say to you.

My poor master. What's become of him now? Where's that part of him that talked and dreamed? Maybe up there in the pure world on the earth's highest plateau—in that realm filled with pure colors that Plato saw and that men call divine. Maybe he's on that terrestrial plane from which precious stones fall, where pure and purified men drink air and breathe ether. That's where the pure dogs are too: Saint Hubert the hunter's dog and Saint Dominic's dog—with his torch in his mouth—and Saint Roch's. Pointing to the saint's image, a preacher used to say, "Here is Saint Roch, with his little dog and all!" There, in that pure Platonic world where ideas are incarnate is where the pure dog resides, the truly "cynical" dog. And that's where my master is.

I feel that contact with this death and my master's purification is purifying my soul, too. My soul is yearning for the fog into which he dissolved, the fog from which he emerged and to which he returned.

Orfeo feels the dark fog coming and runs to his master, jumping and wagging his tail. "Master! Master! Poor man!"

Domingo and Liduvina picked up the dog lying dead at the feet of his master, purified like him and enveloped, like him, in the dark cloud. When Domingo saw the dog, he was deeply moved and wept. No one knows if he cried for his master's death or for the dog's. Most likely he cried at the wondrous sight of such loyalty and fidelity.

"And they say grief never kills," he remarked.